Two Shows for the Price of One . . .

"Anything wrong, dear?" Gina asked.

"No, it's just that high-rise robbery," Mario said. "We thought those marks on the railings of the balcony might lead somewhere, but it was a dead end."

Frank shot a questioning look at Joe.

"I saw Aérocirque's first performance last night," Mario said, "and you all are in for an amazing treat."

"Matt saw them in New York, but it'll be the first time for the rest of us," Tony said. "We can hardly wait!"

Frank was looking forward to the performance too, but the high-rise burglary suddenly seemed more interesting.

The Hardy Boys Mystery Stories

Available from ALADDIN Paperbacks

THE HARDY BOYS®

#189
ONE FALSE STEP

FRANKLIN W. DIXON

Aladdin Paperbacks
New York London Toronto Sydney

This book is a work of fiction. Any references to historical events,
real people, or real locales are used fictitiously. Other names, characters, places,
and incidents are the product of the author's imagination,
and any resemblance to actual events or locales or persons, living or dead,
is entirely coincidental.

First Aladdin Paperbacks edition February 2005
Copyright © 2005 by Simon & Schuster, Inc.

ALADDIN PAPERBACKS
An imprint of Simon & Schuster
Children's Publishing Division
1230 Avenue of the Americas
New York, NY 10020

The text of this book was set in New Caledonia.

Printed in the United States of America
2 4 6 8 10 9 7 5 3 1

THE HARDY BOYS MYSTERY STORIES is a trademark of Simon & Schuster, Inc.
THE HARDY BOYS and colophon are registered trademarks of Simon & Schuster, Inc.

Library of Congress Control Number: 2004106922
0-689-87364-6

Contents

ONE FALSE STEP

1 Aérocirque

"I wish you two could have gone with me to see Aérocirque in New York last Saturday," Matt Jenkins said to Frank and Joe Hardy. "It was amazing!"

"*Aérocirque?*" seventeen-year-old Joe Hardy said. He sprayed some mousse on his blond hair and started combing it in. "I've never heard of it before."

"The New York show was their first," Matt said. "The owner is a rich European who's hired some of the best pilots and aerialists from all over Europe and turned them into 'Aérocirque.'"

Frank Hardy, who was a year older than his brother, pulled a blue sweater over his head, recombed his dark hair with his fingers, and said,

1

"We were in Montreal helping Dad on a mystery case, so we couldn't have gone anyway—but I've never heard of Aérocirque either. It sounds like something Joe and I would really like to have seen. Maybe next time."

Frank and Joe often helped their famous father solve mysteries all over the world. When police departments from Calcutta to Calgary, from Dallas to Dubai were confronted with cases that stumped them, they called on Fenton Hardy—and he called on his sons for assistance.

"Well, I've got a copy of their schedule in my backpack," Matt said, "so if their next performance is not too far from Bayport, maybe we could go."

"Great idea," Joe said.

The three of them headed out of the Hardys' house to Frank and Joe's van.

"I appreciate the ride to school, guys," Matt said. "My car won't be ready for several days. They had to order a part."

"It's no problem," Frank said. "We're glad to have you along."

Matt and his mother had moved into the house next door a couple of weeks before, and Matt had immediately fit in with Frank and Joe and their friends. Dr. Jenkins had just recently retired from the diplomatic service. She had grown up in Bayport and wanted Matt to spent what was left of his high school years there. Matt's father, a well-known mystery writer, had died of cancer when the family was living in Botswana.

Joe looked at his watch: "We're going to be late if we don't hurry," he said. "I didn't finish reading chapter seven in my world history book, and we're going to have a test on it this morning."

"What's the chapter about?" Matt asked.

"The apartheid years in South Africa," Joe said.

"Well, we never lived in South Africa, but Botswana is right next door," Matt said, "so I know all about that period. Apartheid affected all the surrounding countries."

While Frank drove them to school, Matt told Joe all he knew about the South African policy of racial separation from the late 1940s through the 1990s, when Nelson Mandela became the country's first black leader.

As Frank pulled into the student parking lot of Bayport High School, Joe said, "Thanks to you, Matt, I should get an A on that test! We need to do this more often. You're better than a textbook."

"I learned a lot of things about that time too," Frank agreed. "Hey, there's Chet!" Frank gave a short toot of his horn to get Chet Morton's attention. "I need to ask him what the track coach said about tryouts next week. They were talking the other day."

Matt unzipped his backpack. "I got so busy talking about apartheid, I forgot about the Aérocirque schedule," he said. He pulled out a piece of paper.

"Here it is. Hey! They have several performances in Philadelphia this week." He looked up. "We ought to get some of the gang together and go."

"Sounds like a great idea to me," Joe said.

"Let's talk about it at lunch," Frank suggested.

Frank surveyed the crowded cafeteria. "Do you see Joe and Matt?" he asked Chet and Tony Prito, who had just joined him.

"Looks like they're sitting down by Callie and Iola at that back table," Tony said, nodding in their direction, "but there are still three empty chairs."

Iola Morton was Chet's sister and a frequent date of Joe's. Sometimes Iola and Joe double dated with Frank and Callie Shaw.

"Do we *have* to sit with my sister?" Chet said. "I see enough of her at home."

"Don't be so hard on her, Chet," Frank said. "Anyway, I promised Joe and Matt that we'd talk about going to see Aérocirque this weekend."

The three of them headed for the serving line to get their trays.

"I saw some pictures of that in the Sunday news-paper," Tony said. "There were these two helicopters with a wire between them—and this guy was walking it!"

"How can the person keep his balance?" Chet said. "Could you please give me double mashed

4

potatoes?" he asked Mrs. Conroy, one of the cafeteria servers. He gave her a big smile.

"I always give you double servings, Chet," Mrs. Conroy said. "You don't have to ask."

Chet grinned. "Thanks, Mrs. Conroy," he said.

"What about us, Mrs. Conroy?" Tony said. "Frank and I are really hungry too."

Mrs. Conroy shook her head. "Your coach told me you two are in training, so there are no doubles until track season is over," she said. She leaned closer to them. "If you win district, I might even think about tripling your servings."

Frank smiled.

As soon as they got their drinks, Frank, Chet, and Tony headed for the back table.

When they arrived, Frank said, "Hey, Callie! How'd you do on that math test?"

Callie shook her head. "I can't believe I studied so much and knew so little," she said.

Iola rolled her eyes. "That means she must have scored ninety-nine instead of a hundred," she said.

"What were you guys talking about before?" Chet asked. "I hope it's something that will be good for my digestion."

Joe looked at Chet's plate. "I'm not sure *anything* is going to help your digestion if you eat all of that."

"Callie was telling us about a friend of hers in New York City whose family's apartment was robbed Saturday night," Matt said.

5

"Oh, I thought it was something really interesting," Tony said. "Those things happen all the time in big cities."

"This is different," Callie said. "The police are totally stumped."

"What makes this crime so different, Callie?" Frank asked. He tasted the green beans, then moved them to the side of his plate. "Too salty," he said.

"Do you remember Mary Beth Edwards? She's visited me here in Bayport several times," Callie said. "Our families are distantly related in some way."

Joe nodded. "She's the one who looks like she could be your twin sister, right?"

"Right," Callie said. "Well, she and her family live in the apartment just below the penthouse in a new high-rise on West Sixty-ninth Street in Manhattan, and they were robbed Saturday night," she continued. "What makes this so different is that the thieves got in through the French doors off the balcony."

"Window washers!" Tony said.

Callie shook her head. "Nope. The police have ruled that out."

"Maybe it was one of those building climbers," Matt suggested. "You know, the people who'd rather climb up buildings than mountains."

"The police don't think so," Callie responded.

"Anyway, somebody always spots those people before they get to the top."

"Well, there has to be an explanation," Chet said. "It couldn't be somebody who just flew in and landed on the balcony, like one of those superheroes."

"If you're saying that you don't believe in superheroes anymore, Chet, then I guess we can throw away all those old comic books in the attic," Iola said, smiling. "I need more space to store my things."

"Don't you touch those comic books!" Chet said. "They're worth a fortune!"

Everyone at the table laughed.

Callie looked at Frank and Joe. "Mary Beth wanted me to tell you about it," she said. "She was hoping you two could suggest some ideas about who might have committed this crime to the New York police."

"You know, someone they might have missed," Iola added.

"Sure," Joe said. "We'd be glad to."

"We'll also talk to Dad," Frank added. "If I know him, he probably already knows about the case and has some theories of his own."

Matt looked at his watch. "I hate to change the subject, Callie, but we were going to make some plans to go see Aérocirque this weekend in Philadelphia."

"*Aérocirque!* That's where Mary Beth and her parents were when their apartment was robbed," Callie said. "She said she had never seen anything so exciting."

"It was like nothing I had ever seen before either," Matt said. He unfolded a piece of paper and laid it on the table. "Here's Aérocirque's schedule. They'll be in Philadelphia for five days. If we leave Bayport Friday after school, we can see several performances."

"Why do we need to go so many times?" Chet asked.

"Yeah," Tony agreed. "It sounds interesting, but wouldn't one performance be enough?"

"They have several troupes of acrobats," Matt explained. "They don't all perform every night."

"I don't know," Chet said. "I had some other plans for this weekend."

"I hate to be a killjoy," Tony said, "but . . ."

"It won't be as much fun if we don't all go together. I was really looking forward to it," Matt said. He looked around the table. "Look, guys, I'm sorry. I know I come on strong sometimes. You have to understand how much I'm enjoying having a normal American high school experience after spending so much time overseas. But anyway, who knows? Aérocirque will probably be on television in a few months. That'll be just as good."

"Not really," Joe said.

"Well, if we don't want to stay after the show Friday night, we can get up Saturday morning and come back to Bayport," Frank said.

"I guess that would work," Chet said.

Tony nodded his agreement.

"If Mom and Dad don't have a problem with it, then we'll drive down to Philadelphia Friday after school," Frank said.

"You won't regret it, I guarantee it!" Matt said.

They all gathered up their trays and headed for the conveyor belt.

"Don't forget about Mary Beth's robbery," Callie reminded Frank.

"We won't," Frank said. "I promise."

As Frank and Joe headed to the first of their afternoon classes, Joe said, "You know, this is a lot like one of those 'locked room' puzzles that Aunt Gertrude enjoys reading about so much. You know, when a crime is committed in a locked room, and nobody can figure out how it could have happened."

"That could be, Joe," Frank said, "but at the end, the detectives always figure the puzzle out—and I'm sure that's what'll happen this time."

2 Detective Zettarella's Problem

When Frank and Joe got home after school that day they went straight to the kitchen, where Mrs. Hardy had thick slices of chocolate cake and glasses of cold milk ready for them.

"Thanks, Mom!" Joe said. "My favorite!"

"If it's *food* it's your favorite, Joe Hardy!" Aunt Gertrude said, breezing into the kitchen, a finger holding her place in the latest romance novel she was reading. She gave both Joe and Frank a peck on the cheek. "I don't know how you boys can eat so much and stay so slim. I just need to look at a slice of cake to put on ten pounds."

"Exercise," Frank said. "That's the secret."

"We have to eat this much, Aunt Gertrude," Joe added. "If we didn't, we'd be skin and bones."

"I guess so," Aunt Gertrude said.

"Anyway, you're looking great, Aunt Gertrude," Frank said. "It must be all those trips to your new gym downtown."

Aunt Gertrude blushed.

"How's Mr. Phillips?" Joe asked. "Are you and he still dating?"

Aunt Gertrude blushed even deeper. "Good heavens, Joe Hardy! You make it sound like we're a couple of teenagers!" she said. "Mr. Phillips and I are merely friends who enjoy attending an occasional philharmonic concert together." She turned to Mrs. Hardy. "Laura, if you need me to help you with dinner I'll be glad to, but if not, I'd just as soon finish this novel I'm reading."

"Thank you, Gertrude. I have it all under control," Mrs. Hardy said. "Finish your book."

Joe crooked his head so he could read the title. *The Bride from Butte.* He looked at his aunt and grinned. "Sounds interesting," he said. "Are you getting some good ideas from it?"

"Don't you go thinking I'm looking to get married, Joe Hardy," Aunt Gertrude said. "This book was written by the granddaughter of a friend I went to college with. She asked me to read it."

Joe winked at Frank, and Frank grinned back.

After Frank and Joe had had two more pieces of cake each, Frank said, "Mom, we were thinking about driving to Philadelphia this weekend to catch a couple of the Aérocirque performances. Would that be all right?"

Mrs. Hardy took a casserole out of the oven, set it on a wire rack, and said, "We don't have any relatives in Philadelphia, Frank. Where would you stay?"

"I was thinking we could just rent a hotel room, Mom," Frank said. "Several of the guys are going. Matt. Chet. Tony. We could pool our money."

"Matt went to see Aérocirque in New York last weekend, Mom, when were were in Montreal helping Dad," Joe added, "and he can't stop raving about it."

"Is it like that fancy circus that's in Las Vegas all the time?" Aunt Gertrude asked.

"No, this one is always in a big outdoor stadium. It uses helicopters," Joe explained.

"They tie a wire to a couple of helicopters, and then the acrobats walk across it while the helicopters are in the air," Frank added.

"I've never heard of anything so dangerous in all my life," Mrs. Hardy said.

"It's the danger that makes it exciting!" Joe said.

"That's not all," Frank said. "Some of the helicopters have trapezes attached to them on the bottom, and some of the aerialists swing from one to another."

"Oh, my goodness! What is this world coming to?" Aunt Gertrude said. "When I was growing up, we got excited if we saw lions and tigers at the circus."

"Times have changed, Aunt Gertrude," Joe said.

"Well, if you're only planning to watch and not participate, then ask your father and see what he has to say about you going," Mrs. Hardy said. "But it sounds fine to me."

"Dad always tells us to check with you first, Mom," Frank said, "so is it all right if we tell him you think it's a great idea?"

"I didn't say I thought it was a *great* idea, Frank Hardy," Mrs. Hardy said. "I only said, well . . ." She sighed. "All right, just tell him that I thought it was a great idea!"

"Laura, it's probably safer than some of the cases they've been on," Aunt Gertrude said. She turned a page of her romance novel. "Sometimes I wish we lived in a simpler age."

Frank and Joe headed for Mr. Hardy's study. The door was closed, so Frank knocked.

"Come in," Mr. Hardy said.

"Do you have a couple of minutes, Dad?" Joe said. "We have something to ask you."

"I always have time for my sons," Mr. Hardy said. "I'm actually glad for a break. I'm stumped."

"Are you working on another case?" Frank asked.

"Yes, but it's not my case," Mr. Hardy said. "I just got off the telephone with Detective Rodriguez in New York. He wanted my opinion on the robbery of a high-rise apartment."

Frank and Joe looked at each other.

13

"Was the robbery Saturday night, and did the apartment belong to a family named Edwards?" Joe asked.

Mr. Hardy blinked in surprise. "How did you know that?" he asked.

Frank repeated what Callie had told them in the cafeteria.

"Callie said the police think the thieves came in through the French doors off the balcony," Joe added, "but they don't have any evidence."

"Well, that's not quite true. I know you boys won't repeat this—the police did find some strange marks on the railing of the balcony," Mr. Hardy said. "Dr. Edwards said he was sure they weren't there before the robbery."

"When Callie was telling us about the robbery, the first thing I thought of was window washers," Frank said, "but I guess that the police have ruled that out."

Mr. Hardy nodded. "I promised Detective Rodriguez I'd think about it, so that's what I was just doing," he said. "What was it you boys needed to talk to me about?"

Frank told Mr. Hardy about Aérocirque and their plans to go to Philadelphia to attend some of the performances.

"Have you talked to your mother?" Mr. Hardy asked.

Frank and Joe grinned.

"She said it was all right with her if it was all right with you," Joe said.

14

"Well, you'll need a place to stay, so I'm going to call Mario Zettarella," Mr. Hardy said.

"Who's that?" Frank asked.

"He's an acquaintance of mine in the Philadelphia Police Department," Mr. Hardy said.

"We could just rent a hotel room, Dad," Joe said. "We don't want to put people out."

"Nonsense," Mr. Hardy said.

"There are going to be five of us altogether, Dad," Frank added. "That's a lot of people to have as guests."

"The Zettarellas have five sons," Mr. Hardy said. "They're all grown now, but Mario told me the last time I talked to him that he and his wife missed having them around."

Mr. Hardy picked up the telephone and dialed a number. Within minutes, the arrangements were made. "Thanks, Mario, and we hope to see you and Gina in Bayport one of these days." When he hung up the phone, Mr. Hardy added, "It's a good thing I called. Mario said that tickets to the Aérocirque performances are almost impossible to get, but he's on special detail for all the shows, so all five of you guys can go with him."

"Great, Dad!" Frank said. "Well, I guess this is a good example of how things always happen for a reason."

"Let's go next door and tell Matt," Joe suggested.

* * * *

15

On Friday afternoon after school, Frank and Joe picked up Matt, Chet, and Tony.

"We'll head on over to I-95," Frank said as they left the city limits of Bayport. "That's the fastest route to Philadelphia."

"I'm hungry," Chet said. "Do you think we can stop somewhere to eat?"

Matt looked over at Chet. "Are you serious? We haven't been on the road for more than ten minutes."

"I know, I know," Chet said, "but riding in a car makes me hungry."

"It really does, Matt," Joe said. "You should hear Mrs. Morton talk about all their family trips when Chet and Iola were kids."

"It always took them twice as long to get where they were going," Frank said.

"That's why we brought along a cooler of food," Joe said. "We're prepared."

"You guys are great," Chet said. He looked over his shoulder. "Pass it up here."

"It's too big, Chet," Frank said. "Matt, lean over the back seat and get Chet one of those turkey sandwiches on top."

"And something to drink, and some chips," Chet added.

"This is making me hungry too," Matt said. "Is it all right if I help myself?"

"Sure! That's what it's there for," Joe said. "Mom packed enough for an army. I could hardly lift the cooler to get it into the back."

"There's the interchange ahead of us," Frank said. "I-95 goes right into Philadelphia. According to Dad's directions, we need to exit onto the Pennsylvania Turnpike, get off at the Hatboro exit, and then drive south a few miles to Willow Grove." He looked at his watch. "We should get to the Zettarella's house in time to go with Detective Zettarella to tonight's performance of Aérocirque!"

Highway construction in New York and New Jersey and a fifteen-vehicle pileup with no serious injuries just before Frank reached the Pennsylvania Turnpike cut their scheduled arrival time closer than Frank would have liked, but Mr. Hardy's precise directions made the difference. They arrived in front of the Zettarella's house on Haverford Lane at 5:30.

"Great job, Frank," Matt said.

"I'm hungry," Chet said. "I wonder if we're in time for dinner."

"I only ate half of this banana," Tony said. He handed it to Chet. "I'll pass," Chet said, grimacing.

Just then the front door opened, and a man who looked like a professional football player started toward their van.

"I hope that's Detective Zettarella," Matt said. "If it's not, we're in trouble."

The man smiled and waved at them.

17

Joe hopped out of the van. "Detective Zettarella?" he said.

"In the flesh," the man said, grabbing Joe's hand and shaking it vigorously. "But you're not going to spend the whole time you're here calling me 'Detective Zettarella.' It's Mario, okay?"

Joe grinned. "Okay, Mario," he said.

Frank had come up behind Joe. He introduced himself and the rest of the boys.

"Well, Gina, my wife, has fixed a quick meal for us," Mario said, "so let's go inside, because we really do need to leave by six."

Everyone followed Mario into the house.

"Wow! That smells wonderful!" Chet said. "I'm starved."

"You ate most of the food from the cooler, Chet," Matt said. "I'm amazed you have room for anything else."

"Oh, don't worry, Matt," Tony said. "Chet's stomach is a bottomless pit."

"I hope Mrs. Zettarella didn't go to a lot of trouble," Frank said. "We could have just snacked at the circus."

"Trouble? Not at all," Mario said. "Your father probably told you that we reared five boys, and even though they've been gone from home for several years, Gina still misses cooking for a big crowd. When I told her the five of you were coming to stay with us for a few days, she immediately went

18

grocery shopping, and she's been in the kitchen ever since. I haven't seen her this happy in years!"

Mario introduced everyone to Mrs. Zettarella, who gave them each a big hug and told them to call her Gina.

After they had all washed up in the guest bathroom, Mario said, "Okay, boys, let's dig in, and then we'll head on over to the stadium."

Just then Mario's cell phone rang. He identified himself, then, after a couple of minutes, said, "Well, that's too bad. I thought it might lead us somewhere. Okay. I'll see you in the morning."

"Anything wrong, dear?" Gina asked.

"No, it's just that high-rise robbery downtown," Mario said. "We thought those marks on the railings of the balcony might lead somewhere, but it was a dead end."

Frank shot a questioning look at Joe.

"I saw Aérocirque's first Philadelphia performance last night," Mario said, "and you all are in for an amazing treat."

"Matt saw them in New York, but it'll be the first time for the rest of us," Tony said. "We can hardly wait!"

Frank was looking forward to the performance too, but the high-rise burglary suddenly seemed more interesting.

3 The Mystery of the Missing Acrobats

Just then a horn sounded in front of the Zettarella's house.

"Our ride's here, kids," Mario said. "It's two hours before the show starts, but I need to be at the stadium early to check out the security. It'll also give me time to introduce you to some of the performers and to show you what goes on behind the scenes."

Gina popped open a plastic container of moist towelettes. "I'll make hand-washing easy for you, boys," she said with a smile.

Chet gave her a big grin. "My mother would be proud of me," he said as he took one of the towelettes and wiped his hands. "Thanks, Gina."

"Well, when our boys were at home they were

constantly coming and going," Gina said, "so I tried to make life as simple for them as possible."

"Some people might call it 'spoiling,' dear," Mario said with a smile.

"I don't care what some people might call it, Mario," Gina said, smiling. "A mother has the right to spoil her sons."

"If you don't watch it, boys, you'll be forced to have breakfast in bed while you're here!" Mario said. "When our boys were home, it was more like a hotel with room service than a house."

Gina winked at Frank and Joe. "Ask Mario how many times a week he gets breakfast in bed," she said. "Then ask him how many times he's refused it."

Frank noticed Mario blushing.

"Oh, okay, I give up," Mario said. The horn outside honked again. "We have to go. Bill's going to wonder what's taking us so long." He kissed Gina. "You win, dear. We'll see you after Aérocirque."

"Have fun, but be careful, boys," Gina said. "When I think about all those helicopters flying around that stadium, I get very nervous."

"We'll be careful," Frank assured her.

Mario led the way out of the house.

A white van was parked in front. On the side it read PHILADELPHIA POLICE—SPECIAL FORCES.

"Wow! Some wheels!" Joe said. "I wish our van looked like that."

Frank nodded.

Mario got in the front seat beside the driver, and the rest of them climbed into the back. Mario quickly introduced Bill, the driver.

"Are we going to have a problem here?" Bill asked.

Joe thought he sounded really irritated. He looked at Frank and raised an eyebrow.

Frank gave him an almost imperceptible nod. *That's a strange question,* he thought.

Mario shook his head. "No," he said. "Why?"

Without responding, Bill pulled away from the curb and headed out of the neighborhood.

When they reached Highway 263, Bill turned the van north.

"Aérocirque is performing in a brand new stadium just north of Warminster. It was built for several high schools in the area," Mario said. "It's not very far from here."

On the way, Mario talked about how hard it was to get tickets to see Aérocirque. "They're going for two hundred dollars apiece," he said. "Almost everyone in the metropolitan Philadelphia area wants to see it, but unfortunately only people with lots of money can get the tickets now."

"That doesn't seem fair," Joe said.

"Why not?" Bill said, finally breaking his silence. "It's all about making money."

What's this guy's problem? Joe thought.

"It wouldn't surprise me if tickets were going for a thousand dollars a pop by the time Aérocirque reaches Los Angeles," Mario said, looking at Bill. "That's the last city on their tour. You could never pay that kind of money on a cop's salary. It makes me bitter sometimes."

Joe looked over at Frank. He could tell that his brother was also surprised at how much anger they were seeing from Bill, and now Mario, too. It was making him really uncomfortable.

"I wish I could think up something to make that kind of money," Chet said.

"You and me both," Bill said.

Frank noticed he glanced at Mario before he said it.

"Mario, I don't mean to pry, but right before we left you mentioned something about a burglary in a high-rise apartment building in downtown Philadelphia," Frank said. "We were talking to a friend of ours at school on Friday, and she was telling us about a high-rise apartment burglary in Manhattan last week. The New York police are stumped too."

Mario looked at him. "Really? Well, I guess the same kinds of crimes happen in big cities," he said. "These crooks got in through the French doors on the balcony."

"That's what happened in Manhattan, too," Joe said. "The police found some scratches on the railing around the balcony that they couldn't explain."

"Now, that's strange," Mario said. "We found some scratches we couldn't explain either."

"Mario, I don't think it's a good idea to . . ." Bill started to say, but Mario waved him off.

"Sounds to me like some kind of gang is making its way around the country," Matt said.

"Have you checked the police reports in other cities to see if they've had similar robberies?" Frank asked.

"No, we haven't yet, although that's something we usually do if we can't find any clues on our own. Since we're just barely at the beginning of our own investigation, nobody has gotten around to that yet," Mario said. "It sounds to me that these two crimes are similar enough that it might be a good idea to go ahead and do it."

"That must be the stadium up ahead," Tony said. "I see some really bright lights."

"It is," Bill said. "We'll be there shortly."

Just then Joe heard a loud whirling noise over the van, and within a few seconds two black helicopters flew into view.

"Wow! For a minute, I thought they were going to land on top of us," Chet said. "They look like a couple of birds fighting over their territory."

"That's one of the things they do in the show," Matt said. "Once or twice when I was watching, I was just *sure* they were going to hit each other."

24

"I think we're in for a thrilling night," Joe said. "This is going to beat any action movie I've seen lately!"

"I agree," Frank said.

Bill drove into the stadium parking lot and pulled the police van into a reserved spot.

"There's another practice field on the other side of the stadium. You can't see it from here, because it's hidden behind the press box, but that's where the acrobats work on last-minute details before the performances," Mario said. "I need to make sure everything's all right. I thought you'd like a look at what goes on behind the scenes. How about it?"

Everyone agreed that was a great idea.

Several more helicopters began whirling above them as they made their way around the stadium.

"You can feel the excitement in the air, can't you?" Matt said. "I'm glad we got to come to this."

"I'm glad you suggested it," Joe said. When they reached the practice field, Frank saw two of the black helicopters hovering just a few feet above the ground. A wire was stretched between them, and two acrobats were walking the wire toward each other.

"What are they going to do when they meet?" Joe asked.

"Watch," Matt told him.

As the two acrobats continued walking toward each other, the helicopters began to rise slowly.

One acrobat appeared unsteady for a minute, but he finally regained his poise and continued along the wire.

When the acrobats finally reached each other, one slowly squatted on the wire. The helicopters were now at almost the same height as the top of the press box. The acrobat who was still standing suddenly jumped over the squatting acrobat and landed smoothly on the other side. The squatting acrobat stood up and continued toward the other helicopter.

When the acrobats reached the opposite helicopters, they untied the wire, let it fall to the ground, got into the passenger seat, and the helicopters flew away.

Frank let out his breath. "Wow!" he said. "I can hardly wait to see that again!"

"Me too!" Joe said.

"That's just the beginning," Matt said. "It gets even better!"

"Matt's right," Mario said. "These acrobats have nerves of steel."

With Mario in the lead and Frank and Joe right behind him, they all started toward a big tent in one corner of the practice field. It took them about ten minutes to get there.

A couple of police officers were standing at the entrance.

"Everything okay?" Mario asked them.

"Yes, sir," one of the officers said.

Mario introduced the Hardy boys and their friends to the two men. "I'm going to give the boys a behind-the-scenes tour," he said. He looked at his watch. "I'll check out the security in the stadium on the way to our seats."

Both police officers nodded.

Once inside the tent, Frank saw that it had been sectioned off, with acrobats in different-colored costumes practicing their routines on trapezes hanging from scaffolding or on wires just a few feet above the ground.

"Aérocirque has different teams which perform different acts," Mario said. "Over there, you have the trapeze artists, who fly from trapeze to trapeze under hovering helicopters."

"I didn't get to see those in New York," Matt said. "I hope they perform tonight."

"On the other side of them, you have some more aerialists, like the ones you saw earlier," Mario said, "but these guys have to be steady enough to catch other trapeze acrobats who fly through the air and land on their shoulders."

Joe looked at Mario. "Are you serious?" he said. "It sounds like they defy gravity."

Mario nodded. "You have to see it to believe it, Joe," he said.

"This tent is closed to spectators! Get out!"

Frank turned at the sound of an angry and

accented voice. A man in tight-fitting green spandex was watching them, hands on hips.

"It's all right," Mario said. He showed the man his badge. "I'm Detective Zettarella. I'm in charge of security."

"We need water. We need lots of cold water," the man said, ignoring Mario's badge. "You and your boys need to get us some cold water now."

Mario gave the acrobat a hard look. "You have us mixed up with the caterers," he said. He looked around. "Why don't you ask that young lady over there, the one in red? She can help you."

"You go ask her!" the acrobat screamed. "I am an artist, and I don't have time to waste arguing with you."

Frank could tell that Mario was about to explode, so he stepped in. "I'll go," he said. "I could use a cold drink myself. Where do you want the water sent?"

Now the acrobat had a smirk on his face. "Over there!" he said. He pointed to a far corner of the tent, where other acrobats dressed the same way he was were lining up to leave the area. "Hurry!" With that, he turned and ran to rejoin his troupe.

"How arrogant!" Joe muttered. "Who does he think he is, anyway?" He turned to Frank. "Why did you agree to do that? He treated you like his personal servant."

"Don't worry, Joe," Frank said. "I'm not getting the water. And I have my reasons for making nice."

28

"I'm disappointed," Matt said. "Are all the acrobats like that?"

"No, some of them are more like thugs," Mario said. "They're an interesting collection of humans."

Joe looked at Frank. "I suppose it's normal for entertainers to have big egos," he said. "I guess we shouldn't be surprised."

"I guess not, but I've just about had it," Mario said. "Our job is to make sure everyone in this stadium is safe, including the performers—but you'd think they didn't care." He looked at his watch. "We need to head to our seats," he added. "There are some things I have to check out on the way, and it'll take several minutes to make our way through the crowd."

"Hey, guys! Take a look at that girl over there!" Tony said. "She's gorgeous."

Everyone looked.

"Well, you just might get to meet her later," Mario said. "That's Elisabeth von Battenberg, the daughter of the man who owns Aérocirque. In fact, that's the baron standing right behind her. They live here in Philadelphia, in one of the most expensive high-rise apartments downtown." He paused, and a look of concern spread over his face. "I wonder if something's wrong. The baron seems to be arguing with a couple of the acrobats."

"Why don't you check it out?" Chet said. "That way, you could introduce us to his daughter."

Mario grinned. "Eh, it's probably just some artistic disagreement. I think I'll wait," he said. "But we're sitting close to them in the stadium. I'll introduce you later."

Frank and Joe, with Matt, Chet, and Tony behind them, followed Mario out of the tent and onto the floor of the stadium. Some of the acrobats had already assembled at the opposite end, and there were two black helicopters hovering just a few feet above the ground.

Just then the public address system crackled, and a voice said, "High-Wire Troupe B will not perform tonight because of illness."

"Which group is High-Wire Troupe B? Joe asked.

"The group we saw practicing before we went into the tent," Mario said. "I guess one of the acrobats got sick."

Frank didn't think so, but he had no real proof, so he kept quiet. Given what he had seen earlier, though, he suspected there was something more sinister behind it.

4 Another Robbery

Mario directed them toward the fifty-yard line on the north side of the stadium.

"We're sitting in the VIP section," he said.

"Wow!" Matt exclaimed. "In New York, I was in the nosebleed section. This is great!"

"It sure is," Joe agreed. "We'll be right in the middle of all the action!"

Just then four black helicopters, one coming from each direction of the compass—north, south, east, and west—flew into the stadium and met in the middle. There was a collective gasp from the crowd as the helicopters halted just inches from each other.

"I thought they were going to collide!" Tony said. "They must have this timed perfectly."

"That's what it's all about," Mario said. "*Timing.*"

Suddenly, a trapeze was lowered from the bottom of each of the helicopters. The bars were just a few feet above the ground. Four acrobats, two at each end and two on each side, started running toward the trapezes. Four spotlights lit up their orange sequined costumes.

When the acrobats reached the trapezes, they stood on the bars in unison. Slowly, the helicopters began to rise. As they did, the four acrobats began swinging back and forth.

Joe was amazed at how the helicopters were able to stay the same distance from each other as they rose above the stadium floor.

Soon the acrobats were swinging in almost a semicircle. Then all four fell backward, catching the bar with the backs of their knees. Again, everything was done in perfect unison.

Just when Frank thought nothing else could be as spectacular, the acrobats on the north and west sides left their swings and grabbed hold of the hands of the acrobats on the south and east sides.

Again, there was a loud gasp from the audience.

"I can't believe it," Chet managed to say. "Those guys don't have nets!"

"This really is incredible," Joe said.

After swinging together for several minutes, each pair of acrobats flew through the air toward the empty trapezes, grabbed the bars, swung for several more minutes, then the two helicopters with empty trapezes flew closer to the stadium floor. The two bottom acrobats dove toward the empty trapezes and grabbed the bars with their hands.

For the next several minutes, these movements were repeated in various order.

When this troupe's performance was finally over, Joe said, "You really have to know what you're doing, or it's all over. It makes me want to be up there."

"You can have it," Chet said. "I'd probably break the trapeze." He looked around. "Hey, is there a concession stand nearby? All of this tension has made me hungry."

"Well, I'm not hungry, but I *am* really thirsty," Frank said. He turned to Mario. "Is it okay if we go get something to eat?"

Mario nodded. "It'll be a few minutes before the next troupe gets set up," he said, "so I'll show you where the nearest concession stand is. I can make my next rounds at the same time."

"Should somebody stay here and save our seats?" Tony asked.

"Nobody will take them," Mario said. "This section is for people with special passes only."

As Mario started up the concrete steps toward the exit to the next level, Frank said, "I'm still puzzled about High-Wire Troupe B, Joe. Something's just not adding up."

"It could just be artistic temperament, Frank," Joe said. "You saw how that guy acted about the cold water."

"You may be right," Frank agreed. "It wouldn't surprise me if one of the acrobats suddenly decided that he didn't want to go on, so they all didn't go."

"Well, from what I understand, it happens in the movies all the time," Joe said. "One of the stars will just decide he or she doesn't want to work that morning, and the whole film shuts down."

Frank shrugged. "That could be it," he said.

"Hey, check it out!" Matt said. He was pointing to a group of girls sitting in a row of VIP seats near the top of the section. "Wow! I'd say that Philadelphia has some real sights."

"There are some empty seats around them," Tony said. "Maybe we could sit there for a while and see the circus from a different perspective." He waggled his eyebrows.

"Hey, Joe, Frank!" Chet said. "Ask Mario if we can . . ."

Before Chet could finish, Mario stopped and turned back toward the boys. "I need to ask Baron von Battenberg a question," he said. "Come on. I'll introduce you to him and his daughter. They're sitting in the VIP seats."

Frank turned back to Chet, Matt, and Tony. "You guys must be living a charmed life or something," he told them.

"That's us," Tony said.

After Mario had introduced everyone, Baron von Battenberg said, "Elisabeth, would you introduce your friends to these young men?"

"Certainly, Father," Elisabeth said. She gave everyone a big smile. "This is Alice and Heather. We're all in the same class at Wellington School."

The boys nodded.

"Would you care to sit with us?" Elisabeth asked. "We'd love to have you."

"We were headed to the concession stand," Chet said. "Could we bring something back for you?"

Elisabeth surveyed the girls with a look. They shook their heads but offered their thanks.

"Well, I'd love a soft drink," Elisabeth said to Chet. "If it wouldn't be too much trouble. Whatever you're getting."

"Well, maybe some popcorn," Alice said.

"You're making me hungry," Heather said. "Popcorn sounds good to me, too."

Chet blushed. "Okay, we can do this," he said. He looked at Tony. "You want to help me?"

"Sure," Tony said.

"Well, I'll show you where the concession stand is, boys," Mario said, "and then you can come back down here while I make my rounds."

As Chet and Tony started back up the steps behind Mario, Baron von Battenberg said, "Well, this is indeed a great pleasure and an honor to meet the sons of Fenton Hardy. Although your father and I have never met, I am quite familiar with his work. I have many contacts in police departments all over Europe, and his name is mentioned quite often there."

"Frank and Joe have also solved a lot of mysteries," Matt chimed in. "They're almost as famous as their father."

Baron von Battenberg arched an eyebrow. "Oh, really? Well, that's something I'll remember." He looked around at the empty seats. "I apologize for keeping you standing. Have a seat. I'll let you young people share your stories." He looked at his watch. "If you'll excuse me, I need to make a telephone call, and for some reason my cell phone won't work in this area."

He gave them a big smile. "I'll be back shortly."

Frank, Joe, and Matt sat down.

"Tell us about Bayport," Elisabeth said. "I'm not familiar with it."

Joe gave the girls a quick virtual tour of the city.

"It's a great place to live, really," Matt added. "My mom and I just moved there after living all over the world, and I love it."

"If we need something that only a big city has, then we drive to New York," Frank added.

Matt nodded. "In fact, that's where I saw Aérocirque the first time," he said, "but I wasn't this close to the action."

"Frank and I didn't get to see it New York. We were helping our dad with a case in Montreal," Joe said. "That's why we drove down to Philadelphia."

"What do you think of it so far?" Alice asked.

"It's great," Joe said.

"But I'm disappointed that one of the troupes won't be performing," Frank said. "We just saw them practicing earlier, and everything seemed fine."

"Oh, yes, my father mentioned that one of the acrobats had a sudden attack of allergies or something," Elisabeth said. "But the other troupes are just as exciting, and it'll certainly be worth the trip here, I promise."

Just then the sound of trumpets filled the stadium, announcing that another act was about to begin. Spotlights started dancing around the spectators. Then everything went dark for a few seconds. More trumpets sounded, and four white spotlights slowly crept toward the center of the stadium floor.

"Isn't this choreography amazing?" Heather whispered. "That's really why I'm here. I'm hoping to be a spectacle choreographer myself, and I just love to see how other choreographers work."

"I thought choreographers were dancers," Joe said.

"Well, that's what people usually think of when they think of choreographers," Heather said, "but they can also create acts for planes! I'd love to do something like this."

"Here come the choppers," Frank said as two black helicopters flew into the stadium from each end zone.

When they reached the middle, two acrobats dressed in blue sequined leotards raced toward them. As the helicopters hovered about four feet above the stadium floor, the acrobats attached a wire between them. When the acrobats were finished, one helicopter slowly began to climb until the high wire was stretched at an angle.

Once again trumpets sounded, and one of the acrobats mounted the wire by the lowest helicopter.

Slowly that helicopter began to rise. As it did, the acrobat began to slide along the wire toward the second helicopter.

"This is called the 'stair step,'" Elisabeth whispered. "As each helicopter rises, the acrobat slides down toward the other one."

"Hey, Frank! Joe! Where are you?" Chet called out in the darkness. "We're back with the food!"

Alice retrieved a small flashlight from her purse and shone it on the aisle so Chet and Tony could make their way to the box seats.

After Chet had distributed everyone's food and drinks, he said, "We were halfway down the steps when the lights went out, and I almost dropped everything."

"Can you believe the guy sliding down that high-wire?" Tony said between mouthfuls of popcorn. "What a show!"

Now the helicopters seemed to be rising faster, causing the acrobat to slide rapidly along the wire. Suddenly, the acrobat seemed to lose his balance, and the crowd gasped, but the man reached the end of the wire and righted himself against the door of the helicopter.

"That was probably just part of the act," Chet said. "They want people to think they're going to fall."

"I don't know, Chet," Frank said. "That didn't look like part of any act to me."

The helicopters started back down toward the stadium floor with the acrobat sliding back and forth across the wire until both helicopters were just four feet off the ground. The acrobat jumped off to loud cheers from the spectators.

The second acrobat jumped onto the wire, but this time the helicopters began making a circle as they alternated rising above the stadium floor.

"That would make me dizzy," Matt said.

When the helicopters were finally level with the top of the stadium, they started back down. As the second acrobat jumped off, he bowed to the spectators and received another round of thunderous applause.

Just as the stadium lights came back on, Frank saw Mario coming down the aisle toward them. He looked grim.

"I think something's up, Joe," Frank whispered to his brother. He nodded his head toward Mario.

"He doesn't look really happy, does he?" Joe said.

"Hey, guys, we need to go," Mario said when he reached them. "I've got a problem that I need to deal with."

"What's wrong?" Joe asked.

"There's been another robbery of a high-rise apartment downtown," Mario said. He looked at Elisabeth. "Where's the baron?"

"I don't know, Detective Zettarella," Elisabeth said. "He said he had to take care of some business."

"Well, I need to find him," Mario said. "It was your building that was robbed!"

Elisabeth's hand went to her mouth. "Was it our apartment?" she managed to asked.

"No, but it was the apartment just below yours," Mario said. He looked at his notebook. "It's the Winston apartment. He owns several furniture stores in the greater Philadelphia area."

"Oh, I feel so bad for them, because they're such nice people," Elisabeth said.

"How did that happen?" Alice asked. "Elisabeth's building has the best security in the city."

"From what I understand, the thieves got in through a balcony door, just like the robbery last night," Mario said. "There was nothing on the security tapes at all."

Elisabeth looked at the boys. "I don't want to sound callous about this, but I was planning a party for a few of our friends after the performance," she said, "and I'd love to have you there to meet everyone. What about it?"

"That sounds great to me," Tony said. "I love a good party,"

"Me too," Matt said.

"Good. Since Detective Zettarella is headed to our apartment building anyway, you can ride with him, and when you get there, just come up to the penthouse," Elisabeth said. "I'll phone ahead and tell security that you're coming."

"Well, let's hurry before the lights go off for the next performance," Mario said. "I gather you girls don't need a ride," he said.

"No, we came in my car," Elisabeth said. "My father came by himself."

As they all started toward the steps that would lead them out of the stadium, Frank pulled Joe aside and said, "I like a good party too, Joe, but I'm more interested in this mystery. I say when we get to Elisabeth's apartment building, we make our excuses and tag along with Mario."

"I'm with you," Joe said. "We need to find out if these high-rise burglaries are connected in some way."

5 Clues on the Balcony

Through his cell phone, Mario had prearranged with Bill to have the police van meet them at Gate 42, so all they had to do was jump inside. With help from flashing lights and wailing sirens, they made it out of the stadium parking lot and were on the freeway leading to downtown Philadelphia in just a few minutes.

"Have you talked to any of your officers on the scene yet?" Frank asked.

Mario shook his head. "Bill got the call on the radio, and he let me know about it," he said. "On the surface, it sounds like the robbery we had last night, but it could just be a coincidence."

Frank didn't think so, but like all good detectives,

he'd wait until he got to the scene of the crime to make a final judgment.

Highway 611 changed from York Road to Broad Street when they entered Philadelphia County.

"It's a straight shoot downtown," Mario said.

Joe looked out the window. Once he thought he saw a sign for Temple University, but they were zooming past, so he wasn't sure.

Finally they reached downtown Philadelphia. Just past City Hall, Bill turned onto Chestnut Street and headed east.

"That's the building," Mario said.

Frank looked out and saw a gleaming new high-rise soaring into Philadelphia's night sky. There were several police cruisers and vans parked in front. "Wow! It must cost a fortune to live here!" he said.

Mario nodded. "Millions to move in and millions to maintain," he said. "It's way out of my league."

"Yeah, me too," Chet said. "I can only dream about living in a place like this."

"I *do* dream about it," Matt said. "I'd love to live up in the clouds like that."

"It's a little too tall for me. I get dizzy just climbing a ladder," Tony said. "I'm not quite sure I'm up to this party."

"You'll be all right," Joe said. "Just don't look out a window when you guys get up to Elisabeth's apartment."

"Aren't you and Frank coming with us?" Matt asked.

"We'll catch up with you later," Frank said. "You know that Joe and I can't pass up a case."

Bill pulled the police van into the driveway of the apartment building's front entrance. Joe counted ten police officers standing at the door.

As they all got out of the van, Mario said, "I'll get one of those officers to take you boys up to the von Battenberg's penthouse. The girls aren't here yet, I'm sure, but some of the staff will be, putting the final touches on the party preparations."

Mario went up to one of the officers, spoke to him for a few minutes, then motioned for Chet, Tony, and Matt to follow the man.

"Save us something to eat, Chet!" Joe called as they headed toward the penthouse elevator.

"I'll think about it," Chet called back.

The elevator for the five floors below the penthouse was on the opposite side of the lobby. Mario, Frank, and Joe headed in that direction. Mario pushed the up button.

"I'm glad you guys wanted to go with me," Mario said. "I didn't want to embarrass you in front of your friends, but I've been very impressed over the years with how you two have been able to get to the heart of some of the mysteries that have baffled other detectives."

"Well, we've had a great teacher," Frank said.

"Ever since we were little, Dad has always talked to us about the cases he's been on."

Joe nodded. "Once he tried to read us some Mother Goose stories or something like that, but we told him they were boring," he said, "so he went back to telling about the mysteries he was trying to solve."

The elevator doors opened, and the three of them stepped inside. Mario flashed his badge to the operator, who punched in a code for the Winstons' floor.

When the doors opened again, they were in the foyer of the Winstons' apartment. Everywhere Frank looked, he saw money. The Winstons' apartment was something straight out of a Hollywood movie. Well, maybe a Hollywood *detective* movie, he decided, since there were uniformed police officers everywhere.

"Over here, Detective Zettarella!"

Joe looked in the direction the voice had come from and saw a female officer motioning for them.

When they reached her, Mario said, "Frank, Joe, this is Officer Juana Garcia. If anyone in Philadelphia can solve this crime, she can. Juana, Frank and Joe are the sons of an acquaintance of mine, Fenton Hardy of Bayport. I've told you about America's first family of crime detection." He smiled at the boys.

"Oh, yes," Officer Garcia said. She stuck out her

hand for Frank and Joe to shake. "This is a real pleasure."

"It's nice to meet you, too," Frank said.

"Yes, it is," Joe added.

Officer Garcia turned to Mario. "The Winstons were at the Aérocirque performance. Mr. Winston got ill, so they left in the middle of the show," she said. "We think they just missed coming in during the middle of the robbery."

Mario shook his head. "Well, I guess we and the Winstons should consider ourselves fortunate," he said. "We could have had a robbery-homicide instead of just a robbery."

Officer Garcia nodded grimly.

"Did you find any scratch marks on the railings of the balcony?" Frank asked.

Officer Garcia blinked. "As a matter of fact, we did, but how did you know about that?" she said. "That information hasn't been released yet." She looked at Mario. "Oh, of course. You probably have been talking about this case with Frank and Joe." She turned back to the Hardy boys. "Frankly, we're stumped."

"Well, the main reason Frank and I are interested in the marks is because there was a similar robbery in New York last Saturday night, and there were marks on those railings too."

Officer Garcia raised an eyebrow. "Do you think there might be a connection?" she asked.

"The New York City police seemed convinced they had something to do with how the apartment was robbed," Frank said.

"Instead of just talking about these scratch marks, let's take a look at them," Officer Garcia said. "That's actually why I was motioning to Mario."

They followed Officer Garcia through the Winstons' massive apartment to the French doors which led to the balcony.

"Mrs. Winston said that these doors are never locked," Officer Garcia said. "But really, who expects thieves on the fifty-second floor?"

"What about window washers?" Joe asked.

"There are none," Officer Garcia replied. "Every window in this building can be washed from inside the apartments. Each family's staff takes care of that chore."

Frank turned to Mario. "What about the building that was robbed last night?" he asked.

"It does have window washers, but we've checked that all out," Mario replied. "They were washing the other side of the building, and there was no way any of the workers could have committed the crime."

"It was the same story in New York," Joe offered. "I immediately suspected window washers, but unless there's a window washing gang that's figured out a way to fool the police, that solution won't hold water."

"The scratch marks are over here," Officer Garcia said.

Frank saw the marks from several feet away. "They're bigger than I thought they'd be," he said.

"Me too," Joe said.

"They look exactly like the marks on the balcony at the Fulsome apartment," Officer Garcia said. "The one that was robbed last night," she added.

When they got to the end of the balcony, Mario ran his fingers across the marks. "They're about the same depth as the ones on the Fulsome apartment too," he said. "There's no doubt in my mind now that this was done by the same thieves."

"I'd say the marks were made by a grappling hook of some kind," Frank said. He looked around the balcony, then up toward the top of the apartment building. "A helicopter could have landed on the roof, and the thieves climbed down onto the balcony." He turned to Mario and Officer Garcia. "Has that been checked out?"

"Well, no, actually, it hasn't been," Mario said, "but I'm not sure I'm following you. How does a grappling hook come into the picture?"

"They could have used it to escape," Joe said.

"It would have to be a mighty long rope to reach the ground," Mario said. "I don't know."

"Maybe it didn't have to reach the ground," Frank said. "Maybe it only had to reach the balcony of one of the apartments below this one."

Mario thought for a minute. "Are you suggesting that another resident of the building might be in on this?" he said. "I don't guess that was even a part of the equation for us yet." He looked at Officer Garcia. "Was it?"

Officer Garcia looked embarrassed. "Not yet," she replied. She looked at Frank and Joe and shook her head in amazement.

"I just thought of something else," Joe said. He leaned over the balcony. "It might be a good idea to check for grappling marks on some of the balconies below this one. Let's say no one else in this apartment building is involved. The thieves could simply have stair-stepped down the building."

"What do you mean?" Officer Garcia asked.

"Maybe the rope was just long enough to reach a couple of balconies below," Joe explained. "The thieves could have hooked it to the Winston's balcony, climbed down to the end of the rope, released the hook somehow, then attached it to the balcony they were on and finished climbing down the building that way. People normally don't go around checking their balcony railings for scratch marks, so they may not have noticed them yet."

"Well, maybe they didn't use a helicopter to land on the roof," Mario said. "Maybe that's how they reached the apartment in the first place—by climbing from balcony to balcony."

"Somehow I don't think so, Mario," Frank said.

"Too risky—they'd be seen for sure. I'm surprised they weren't seen earlier. This is all just speculation, anyway, but if they did climb down this way, I think it was only a backup plan. The Winstons arrived home earlier than they were supposed to."

"Well, we've got a lot of theories here, so I think we should start checking them out," Mario said. "Let's start with Air Traffic Control to find out what helicopters were in the downtown area tonight about the time of the robbery."

"I'll get right on it," Officer Garcia said. She headed back through the French doors, leaving Mario alone on the balcony with Frank and Joe.

"Well, guys, I think we've got our work cut out for us," Mario said. "These thieves are really clever, and I have a feeling we've not seen the last of them."

"I've got all these different pieces of the puzzle going around in my head," Frank said, "and I'm trying to put them all together."

"Once we can eliminate some of the theories we've come up with, things will be clearer, I think," Joe added.

"Definitely," Mario said. He looked at his watch. "Well, I need to meet up with the rest of my officers to see what else they've found in the apartment."

"You mean like fingerprints?" Frank said.

Mario nodded. "I really don't expect there to be

any evidence, though," he said. "There was nothing at the other apartment except for the marks on the balcony." He looked at his watch. "Why don't you guys go on up to the von Battenberg's apartment and enjoy yourselves for a while—at least until I finish here? You shouldn't spend all of your time in Philadelphia trying to solve our crimes."

"Well, actually, I can't think of anything I enjoy more than solving mysteries," Joe said, "but if we don't at least show up at the party, we'll never hear the end of it from Matt, Chet, or Tony."

"That's the truth," Frank said.

As they headed toward the elevator that would take them to the von Battenberg's penthouse, Frank decided that one of the first things he wanted to find out was how much Elisabeth knew about the acrobats in Aérocirque.

6 Case Closed?

When the elevator doors opened at the foyer of Baron von Battenberg's penthouse apartment, Frank and Joe were greeted by a huge crowd of young people lit by strobe lights. They were all dancing to loud music. The contrast between the scene in the Winston's apartment and what was now in front of them was shocking.

"Well, life goes on, doesn't it?" Frank said.

"Guess so!" Joe said. "This party was planned before the Winston's robbery, so I guess that Elisabeth didn't see any reason to cancel it."

"I wonder where Chet, Tony, and Matt are," Frank said.

"If we find the food, we'll find Chet," Joe said,

"and if Tony and Matt aren't with him, he can probably tell us where they are."

"We may have to dance our way there, Joe," Frank said as he surveyed the barrier of people in front of them.

"Hey! There's nothing wrong with that," Joe said. "Let's do it!"

Frank and Joe plunged into the crowd. By the time they finally reached a long buffet table, they had each danced with several girls and had been invited to a month's worth of parties all around the Philadelphia area.

"Whew!" Frank said. He took out a handkerchief and wiped his brow. "That was more exhausting than a 5K."

"Yeah," Joe said. He surveyed the array of food. "I think I worked up a hearty appetite."

"Me too," Frank said. He picked up a plate. "You know, I'm surprised Chet isn't standing here."

"I'm not," Joe said. "This place is huge, so there are probably many more tables of food strategically placed."

"You're right," Frank agreed. He helped himself to some chips and a delicious-looking artichoke and spinach dip. "Mmm! This is really good. I think I'm . . ." He stopped in mid-sentence. "Look, Joe. There's Elisabeth von Battenberg, and that guy she's with looks familiar."

Joe looked. "Isn't he one of the acrobats from High-Wire Troupe B?" he said.

"It's hard to tell with the strobe lights," Frank said.

"Well, I think he is," Joe said, "and it looks like he and Elisabeth are arguing about something."

"I say we go check it out, Joe," Frank said. "If it is one of those acrobats from High-Wire Troupe B, I'd like to hear his excuse about why they didn't perform tonight."

The Hardy boys handed their plates to a server and once again plunged into the crowd.

Several times they were stopped by girls wanting to dance with them, but Frank and Joe both managed to make sure that while they were dancing, they were still heading toward Elisabeth and the Aérocirque acrobat. But when they finally reached Elisabeth, the acrobat had disappeared.

Elisabeth gave them a big smile. "Oh, you made it! I'm delighted."

"Yes! It's some party!" Frank said.

"I was afraid you might find the Winston's apartment more interesting," Elisabeth said. She gave them a playful pout. "I would have been really disappointed if one of my parties had come in second to a robbery."

Joe looked around. "Frank and I thought we saw some of the Aérocirque acrobats here talking to you," he said.

Elisabeth looked puzzled. "Oh, really? No, but Daddy may have let them know they were welcome to come to the party, so some of them could be here," she said, once again giving them a wide smile. "I haven't seen any of them." She grabbed Frank's arm. "Come on. I want to introduce the famous Hardy boys around," she said. "Almost every girl here is from a family worth millions of dollars. It'll be worth your while!" Elisabeth stopped. "See that girl with the really red hair?"

Frank and Joe looked.

"Now, that's *red* hair," Frank said.

"It's her natural color, too," Elisabeth said. "That's Julia Baker. She's the heiress to the Baker fortune. They're in oil. She's worth almost a billion dollars."

"Wow!" Joe said.

"That blonde with her is Gretchen Wall. Her family is almost as wealthy as Julia's," Elisabeth said. "They're best friends. They go everywhere together."

The girls suddenly disappeared from their view.

"Oh, Julia is so hard to keep up with," Elisabeth said. "I'll just have to introduce you to—"

"Wait—we probably need to report to our friends from Bayport first, so they won't be wondering where we are," Joe said, interrupting her.

"Have you seen them?" Frank asked.

"No, but that doesn't mean anything," Elisabeth said. "When we got back from the stadium I had a headache, so I lay down for a few minutes, and I only just got up. They're probably with Alice and Heather."

Frank felt that Joe wanted to talk to him alone, so he said, "We'll see if we can find them, then we'll catch up with you later."

"Okay," Elisabeth said.

When Frank and Joe were several feet away, Joe said, "I guess our eyes were playing tricks on us. But I was positive that guy was one of the acrobats from Troupe B."

"Me too," Frank said.

"Something else bothers me, Frank. Why would Elisabeth want us to know how rich all these girls here are?" Joe continued. "Does she think we're fortune hunters?"

"That was a little strange and uncouth," Frank said. "But some people are only impressed by things like that."

Joe nodded. "Let's go find Chet, Matt, and Tony," he said.

The Hardy boys headed through the crowd once again, but this time they ignored every invitation to dance. They slowly made their way through several more rooms, but they didn't see their friends.

"Let's keep going," Frank said.

"Where?" Joe asked. "This place is really big, but there can't be too much more of it."

"I need some air," Frank replied. "I'm hoping the balcony is this way."

Using his height, Frank managed to look over the heads of most of the people in the crowd and finally spotted a set of open French doors. He was also beginning to feel a cool breeze. "I think we're headed in the right direction," he said.

"Hey, there's Chet!" Joe shouted to him. "You were right! He's standing by another refreshment table."

"There's a little more air in this part of the penthouse, so I'm all right," Frank said. "Let's go check in with Chet and see what he and Tony and Matt have been up to."

Once again they had to turn down a couple of invitations to dance, but they finally reached the refreshment table.

"Hey!" Chet called when he saw them. "You won't believe the food at this party!"

"Yes, we would," Joe said. "We've already checked out another table."

"I'm on my fifth table! Each one has different things on it," Chet said with a grin. "I never knew there were so many different kinds of food." He licked some crumbs off his lips.

"I find that hard to believe," Frank said. "Where are Matt and Tony?"

"The last time I saw them, they were with Alice and Heather," Chet said. "Did you know that some of the Aérocirque acrobats were here?"

Joe looked at Frank. "Yeah—Elisabeth was telling us they might be," he said. He turned back to Chet. "Did you recognize any of them?"

"What do you mean?" Chet said.

"Someone was arguing with Elisabeth just a few minutes ago. We thought he was a member of High-Wire Troupe B," Frank said. "When we asked her about it, though, she said she hadn't seen any of the acrobats here."

Chet shrugged. "I thought some of the guys here at the party looked like the acrobats we saw in the tent too, but I haven't seen Elisabeth, so I wouldn't know if she talked to any or not," he said. "The party was already in full swing when we got here, and when we finally saw Alice and Heather, they said that Elisabeth was lying down."

"There they are!" Joe said.

Frank looked, expecting to see Matt and Tony, but instead he saw a couple of the Aérocirque acrobats. They were dancing with Alice and Heather.

"I wonder what happened to Matt and Tony," Chet said.

"Nothing, we're right here," Tony said.

Frank and Joe turned around to find Matt and Tony grinning at the three of them.

"Is this a party or what?" Matt said. "Wow! I haven't had this much fun in months!"

"I see that Alice and Heather dumped you guys," Chet said.

"Yeah, right," Tony said. "They introduced us to a couple of their friends, and we danced with them, and then they introduced us to a couple more of their friends, and now I think we've danced with every girl here."

"Some of the Aérocirque acrobats are here too," Matt said. "We've talked to a couple of them. They acted pretty friendly, nothing like that guy in the tent—you know, the one who ordered us to get him ice water?"

"Cool. Frank and I wanted to talk to them too," Joe said. "What are you guys planning to do now?"

"Go back to dancing," Matt said. "We just happened to see you, so we thought we'd come over here and find out about the robbery."

Joe told them what they had learned in the Winstons' apartment. "We saw the scratch marks on the balcony," he said when he finished. "Mario said they were just like the ones on the balcony of the apartment that was robbed last night."

"I have a feeling they're just like the ones on that apartment balcony in New York, too," Frank added.

"Well, you two must be thrilled that you've got a mystery to solve," Chet said. "Feels just like home, huh? I know I'm happy that I'm completely surrounded by food and nobody is telling me not to eat so much! Unlike home—in the best way."

Frank looked at his watch. "Mario said he'd call me on my cell phone when he was ready to leave the Winstons' apartment," he said, "so you guys go on and do what you want to, and Joe and I'll do some sleuthing. There are several things that we want to check out."

"That sounds like a plan," Matt said. "Our cell phones are on too, so just give us a call when it's time to leave."

Just as Frank and Joe started to leave their friends, they saw some of the Aérocirque acrobats.

"Come on, Joe. They look like they're heading for the balcony," Frank said. "I really want to hear why High-Wire Troupe B didn't perform tonight."

"I'm with you," Joe said.

As the acrobats started toward the rear of the penthouse, Frank saw Julia Baker and Gretchen Wall pass them. The two acrobats stopped and looked. One of them pointed. Frank was sure he mouthed the words "Julia Baker and Gretchen Wall." The other acrobat said something which caused both girls to stop and look back. The acrobats walked up to them and said something that made both girls smile. After a few minutes, they started dancing to one of the few slow dance songs the Hardy boys had heard that evening.

"That's weird, Frank," Joe said.

"Yeah," Frank said. "How would two guys in a circus that's only been in town for a couple of days know the names of two of the richest girls in Philadelphia?"

"I don't know," Joe said. "Maybe Elisabeth introduced them."

60

"Maybe," Frank said.

"I think we need to get closer, so we can hear what they're talking about," Joe said.

The Hardy boys had only gone a few feet when once again they were intercepted by dance partners who didn't seem to notice that Frank and Joe moved them through the room until they were dancing next to the two couples who were their intended destination.

"Now, take Julia's mother, for instance," Gretchen was saying. "She's really nice, but she's also a little odd, because she keeps all of her diamonds under the mattress in their bedroom."

"Really?" the acrobat said.

"Yes, really," Gretchen said.

"Why doesn't she put them in some bank vault?" the acrobat asked.

"She likes to look at them all the time," Gretchen said.

"Isn't that dangerous?" the acrobat asked.

"Why would it be dangerous? They live in the penthouse of another high-rise apartment here in the city," Gretchen said. "Nobody could possibly get in to rob them!"

"I guess you haven't heard about all the high-rise apartment robberies," the acrobat said. "What if one of the crooks happened to overhear you talking about this?"

"Oh, all of Julia's friends know about it, so it's no

big secret," Gretchen said. "Anyway, my father said they were inside jobs. He's sure the help is responsible for what happened, no matter what the police say."

"Really?" the acrobat said.

Gretchen nodded. "I know it's strange, but both the Winstons and the Fulsomes had just fired their limousine drivers," she said. "Since the drivers were friends of each other, my father thinks they planned the robberies together."

Frank and Joe looked at each other.

Frank moved his dance partner around so he could whisper in Joe's ear. "Anyone smell a clue?" he joked.

7 Can Elisabeth Be Trusted?

"But where does the New York robbery fit in?" Joe asked. "That's a bit of a stretch, to think that two limo drivers in Philadelphia might know a limo driver in New York—if there even *was* a driver."

"Oh, I think anybody who lives in an apartment that expensive probably doesn't drive himself or herself anywhere in the city," Frank countered. "I have no doubt they have a driver."

"Yeah, Frank, but—" Joe started to say, but he was interrupted by Frank's cell phone.

Frank looked at the screen and said, "It's Mario." He pushed the receive button and said, "Hello! Okay. I'll round up everyone, and we'll be right down."

"Time to go?" Joe said.

Frank nodded. "I can't believe it's almost two A.M. Let's find the guys and head out," he said. "I'm getting a headache, but I also want to tell Mario what we just overheard."

"Hey! Hey! We were wondering where you were!"

Frank and Joe turned to see Alice and Heather.

"Neither one of you has danced with me," Alice said. She started moving to the music. "This is one of my favorites. Come on, Joe!"

"Detective Zettarella just called, Alice, and we have to leave," Joe said. "I promise I'll dance with you next time."

"Call him back and tell him the party is just starting," Alice said. "One of us can take you home."

"Well, that sounds great, but Detective Zettarella's expecting our help in solving this robbery," Frank said. "There are some things we need to talk to him about."

Alice and Heather both looked disappointed, but Heather said, "Okay, but on one condition!"

"What's that?" Joe asked.

"You told me at the stadium that you'd like to see historic Philadelphia," Heather said, "so tomorrow afternoon you have to let me and Alice take you on a tour."

"Well, I'm not sure that we—" Frank started to say.

But Joe stopped him with "That's a great idea!" He took out a piece of paper, wrote down the

Zettarella's address, and handed it to Heather.

"This will be fun. I like showing friends our city's history," Heather said. "We'll pick you up at noon, so we can have lunch at this little restaurant downtown that's a favorite of ours, and then we'll take a tour of the historic district."

"We'll be ready," Frank said, "but lunch is on us."

"Ah, you are the gentlemen," Alice said, "but we invited, so we're paying, and don't argue because we're very liberated women."

Joe grinned. "All right," he said.

Heather and Alice gave them big smiles and disappeared into the crowd.

Frank and Joe headed back toward the refreshment table where they had last seen Chet.

"Okay, Joe," Frank said. "I'm sure you have a reason besides your interest in American history for being so quick to accept their invitation."

"You bet I do," Joe said. "They're friends of Elisabeth's, and I think we need to find out more about her. Something just isn't adding up."

"I don't know, Joe. I've decided that she's probably just a social climber," Frank said. "I think if the police talk to those two drivers, the Philadelphia robberies *might* be solved."

"But that would make the New York robbery just a coincidence," Joe said.

Frank shrugged. "It happens," he said. "We'll see what Mario has to say."

When they reached the refreshment table, they were in luck. Chet, Tony, and Matt were standing there, eating and talking to three girls.

Frank tapped Matt on the shoulder. "Mario called. He wants us to meet him in the lobby," he said. "We have to leave."

Joe was astonished to see how fast the three of them got rid of their plates, said their good-byes, and led the way out of the apartment.

When they got to the elevators, Frank said, "What was that all about? I've never seen any of you guys leave a party so fast."

"You weren't there to listen to their songs!" Matt said.

"*Songs?*" Joe said.

"Yeah. All three of those girls want to be country-and-western singers," Chet said. "They were trying out some of the songs they'd written."

"Totally awful!" Tony said. "I was getting a headache."

"We didn't want to be rude and just leave in the middle of one of their songs," Matt said, "so when you said it was time to go, it was like the answer to a prayer."

Just then the elevator arrived.

"Well, I'm glad we arrived in time," Frank said.

Mario was waiting for them when the elevator doors opened. Bill had pulled the police van up to the front of the building, so they all got in, and Bill headed back the way they had originally come into the city.

As they drove north on Broad Street, Mario said, "Well, we're stumped, guys. We found nothing new to help with the investigation."

"Joe and I uncovered something," Frank said. "Did you know that the limousine drivers of both of the victims' families knew each other, and that both drivers were fired last week?"

Frank heard Mario's intake of breath. "What?" he said.

"We overheard one of the girls at the party talking about it," Joe said. "She said that her father was sure it had to be the drivers."

Mario got out his cell phone, punched in a number, and in a few seconds said, "Juana? Are you still at the Winstons'? Good. I want you to find out about their limousine driver. He and the Fulsomes's driver may be friends. They were both also fired last week. There could be some connection. Okay. Yes. Call me when you get through. I don't care what time it is." He quickly hung up.

For a while Mario seemed lost in his thoughts, so Frank and Joe didn't disturb him. But when they left the Philadelphia city limits, Mario spoke up. "Well, how was the party?"

Matt started telling him what an incredible apartment the von Battenbergs had, Chet followed with a detailed account of all the food that had been available, and Tony recited the names, addresses, and telephone numbers of close to fifty girls who were there. He'd written them all on scraps of paper.

"They just kept giving them to me," Tony said, stuffing the papers back in his pocket. "I told them I didn't live in Philadelphia, but that didn't seem to matter. They said that the next time I was in town, I should give them a call, and they'd tell me where the best parties were."

"Wow! I should have been dancing more," Matt said. "I was too busy checking out the apartment design. I'm going to be an architect."

"Heather and Alice want to show us historic Philadelphia tomorrow," Joe said. "They're picking us up at noon."

"Not me. I'm not getting up until the middle of the afternoon," Chet said. "I've already seen the Liberty Bell!"

"Well, I haven't, but I'll catch it next time," Tony said. "I don't want to fall asleep at Aérocirque."

"I guess I won't go either," Matt said. "There's nothing more embarrassing than being a fifth wheel."

"It's not a date, Matt, it's just a walking tour of downtown Philadelphia," Joe said. "You're more than welcome. I think Heather and Alice were expecting all of us to go."

"Well, I hope they won't be disappointed, but I think I'll pass," Matt said.

Frank didn't press the issue. Joe made him realize that his initial suspicions about Elisabeth might have been on target. If it were just the four of them, Heather and Alice might open up with some details about her that would answer some of their questions.

The restaurant Heather and Alice took the Hardy boys to was so tiny that it only held about twenty people. It was down a narrow street, almost an alley, off Chestnut Street. It was called Betsy Ross's Kitchen.

"My parents have had a standing reservation for this day every month for years, but I told them I wanted to take the famous Hardy boys, so they agreed to wait until next month to eat here," Alice said. "After you've eaten your meal, you'll realize what a sacrifice my parents made for you."

"Even though it's in the middle of all the things that tourists see, very few tourists know about it," Heather added, "and even if they did, they're usually not here long enough to get a reservation."

When the waiter came, Frank suggested that Alice and Heather order for them. When the meal came, both Frank and Joe pronounced it absolutely remarkable.

When they had finished their desserts, Alice looked at her watch and said, "Well, we need to start the walking tour. I just remembered a doctor's appointment I have later this afternoon." She shrugged. "Sorry."

"That's okay," Joe said. He folded his napkin and laid it on the table. "Are you sure you won't let us pay for this?"

"I'm positive," Heather said. "My father has an account here. It's taken care of."

The four of them exited the restaurant and walked back up to Chestnut Street.

Over the next hour they visited the Liberty Bell, Independence Hall, and Old City Hall.

At Carpenters' Hall, Alice said, "This is where John Adams, Patrick Henry, George Washington, and the other delegates formed the First Continental Congress in 1774."

"You could say this is where America began," Heather added. "It gives me goose bumps just thinking about it."

Last night at Aérocirque and later at Elisabeth's party, Joe thought, Heather and Alice never once struck him as being interested in anything but having a good time. For the next hour, though, they gave Frank and Joe more information about American history, or at least Philadelphia's part in it, than they often got in some of their classes at school. It was interesting.

After stopping for a few minutes at the Philadelphia Visitor's Center, they continued on to the

Betsy Ross House. From there, they stopped at Benjamin Franklin's grave site to pay tribute to him.

"This is great," Joe said. "Frank and I had never been to Philadelphia before."

"I find that hard to believe," Heather said.

"Me too," Frank agreed. "We've been to almost every place else in the world."

"I'm also glad that Philadelphia has a mystery for you to solve," Alice said. "How's it going?"

"Mario had already left for the office by the time we got up this morning," Joe said, "so we don't know if there have been any new developments."

Frank was amazed that neither he nor Joe had mentioned Elisabeth von Battenberg to Heather and Alice yet. They were having such a pleasant time that he had forgotten to do it, but just as he was about to broach the subject, he stopped and looked down the street. "Is that Elisabeth?" he asked.

Joe, Heather, and Alice turned in the direction Frank was looking. "It looks like her to me," Joe said. "Who's that she's with?"

"Looks like some of the acrobats from Aéro-cirque Troupe D," Alice said.

When neither Alice nor Heather said anything else, Frank said, "Do you want to go say hello?"

"No!" Heather said.

Frank and Joe gave her a surprised look.

"We're having too much fun, and she's with

71

someone, anyway," Alice said. "Do you mind if we don't?"

"No, not at all, but I thought the three of you were friends," Frank said.

Heather took in a deep breath and let it out. "We've never really been friends," she said. "Elisabeth came to our school last year, and she was fun because she had lots of good stories about life among Europe's lesser royalty."

"Europe's *lesser* royalty?" Joe said.

Alice nodded. "You know, the kings and queens and princes and princesses without a country to rule," she said. "Elisabeth's family hasn't been in power for hundreds of years, and even when they *were* in power, they only ruled over a small part of Germany. But it's still interesting to hear about."

"But lately she's been acting kind of weird," Heather said. "I think it started when her father put together Aérocirque and brought it over for its American tour."

"It did. That's all she talked about," Alice said. "After Aérocirque arrived in Philadelphia, all she wanted to do was hang around with the acrobats."

Heather shuddered. "I think they're all kind of creepy."

"She told us last night at the party that she didn't really know any of the acrobats that well," Frank said.

"That's not true. In fact, that's about all she wants

to do anymore—hang around with them," Alice said, "but Heather and I aren't interested."

Frank looked down the street. Elisabeth and the acrobats were heading in the opposite direction. "Maybe she just wants to show them historical Philadelphia, like you're doing for us," he said.

"Well, she's going the wrong way," Heather said. "That's where all the new high-rise apartments are."

Joe strained to see down the street. It looked like Elisabeth was pointing to the top of one of the apartment buildings. Suddenly, he had a chilling thought. Would the next robbery take place there?

8 Tipped Off!

"How can you be sure those guys are from High-Wire Troupe D?" Frank asked.

"Well, when Elisabeth first told us about Aéro-cirque, she made the acrobats sound so romantic," Heather said. She rolled her eyes. "I can't believe we were so naïve back then."

"She had pictures of them in her room, and one night when we had a sleepover, she showed us tapes of their practices in Europe," Alice added. "Her father had filmed them according to their speciality, and we just sort of got to know them."

"On tape, they did look handsome and muscular," Heather said, "but in real life, well, they're mostly real creeps."

Joe looked at Heather and Alice. "Will we see you at tonight's performance?" he asked.

"Well, we hadn't planned to go, even though Elisabeth is expecting us to," Alice said, "but we'll go if you guys are planning to be there."

Heather took a deep breath. "We were actually planning to break off our friendship with Elisabeth today," she said, "but I guess we can stand her one more night."

"We'll make sure you're not alone with her," Frank said. "We won't let you out of our sight."

"Frank Hardy, I plan to hold you to that," Alice said.

When Heather and Alice dropped Frank and Joe off at the Zettarella's house, Chet, Matt, and Tony were just having breakfast.

"I haven't felt this great since . . . I don't know when," Matt said. "This is the life!"

"Are you two hungry?" Gina asked as she piled more pancakes on Chet's plate.

"No, we had a really great *lunch* at Betsy Ross's Kitchen," Frank said, looking at Chet. "We'll probably wait until *dinner* to eat again."

"Well, if you get hungry before that, just say something, and I'll fix it for you," Gina said. She gave them all a big smile. "I haven't felt this happy since our boys were home." She shook her head.

"I'm sure that probably sounds silly to you, but I enjoyed being a mother more than I ever enjoyed stocks."

"*Stocks?*" Joe said.

Gina nodded. "When Mario and I met, I worked for one of the big brokerage houses downtown," she said. "I was making a lot of money buying and selling stock for my clients."

"That's great," Frank said.

"Well, my clients and my colleagues thought I was crazy when I married a police officer and moved out to the suburbs," Gina said. "I wouldn't recommend it for everyone—but I made the right decision for myself."

Just as Chet, Matt, and Tony finished breakfast, Mario arrived home from work. "Well, we struck out on the drivers," he said to Frank and Joe. "They knew each other all right, but they both have alibis for the nights of the robberies. And frankly, after what I heard from the officers who talked to them, the two men are closer to being saints than crooks."

"Really?" Joe said. "Why would Gretchen Wall's father make up a story like he did?"

"People *love* conspiracies," Mario said. "I really shouldn't have reacted the way I did, thinking that somebody was hiding something from us, because I know better. It's just that, well . . . we're feeling the pressure because of who's being robbed. These people are movers and shakers in the city. If we don't arrest somebody soon, we're the ones who are going to be moved and shaken, if you know what I mean!" He let out a big sigh. "Enough of that, though. Are you boys ready for another Aérocirque performance?"

"Sure thing," Joe said.

"Well, I need to wash up, but then we'll leave," Mario said. "I'm driving the van tonight. Bill pulled another detail."

Everyone was waiting in the police van when Mario finished getting ready. Frank made sure he had the front passenger seat, because there were some things that he wanted to ask Mario on the way to the stadium. Joe was in the seat behind him.

When they were finally on Highway 611 headed north to the stadium, the time seemed right to Frank to start questioning. "What do you know about Baron von Battenberg and his daughter?"

"What do you mean?" Mario said.

"Are they really as wealthy as everyone thinks they are?" Frank asked.

"What are you getting at?" Mario said.

Joe leaned forward. "Elisabeth seems fascinated by all the money her friends have. She talks about it constantly," he said. "If her father were really as wealthy as everyone thinks, would she be doing that?"

"Maybe rich people like to talk about their money," Mario said. "You're really asking the wrong person."

"Well, it's not so much that she's just talking about it, Mario, it's the way she's talking," Frank said. "She sounds almost envious—as if she wants what she doesn't have."

"I don't know how we could find out without checking the von Battenberg's bank accounts," Mario said, "and at this point, I can't think of a reason why a judge would let me do that."

Frank leaned back. "Yeah . . . I can't either," he said.

"Judges don't consider hunches as solid evidence," Joe added, "and that's about all it is at this point."

"Tell me about it," Mario said.

They rode the rest of the way to the stadium in silence, but Frank's mind was mulling over all of the suspicions that were developing in his head. He was trying to get them in some kind of order.

Joe was doing the same. It was weird how it all worked too. Since he had been around mysteries all his life, certain events, certain things that people said worked their way into his subconscious where they mingled together. Then, all at once, something that hadn't made sense suddenly *did* make sense, and he was on to a possible solution to the crime. He knew that that's what was happening to him now, and probably to Frank, too. He sensed it wouldn't be long until they cracked this case.

Mario parked the police van right at gate forty-two and motioned to one of the police officers who was helping with crowd control. "Everything okay?" he asked.

"Yes, sir, but every seat in the house is taken," the police officer said. "That Baron von Battenberg is going to be richer than he already is!"

Frank and Joe looked at each other.

"I think you and I must be in the minority, thinking that they don't have as much money as everyone thinks they do," Frank whispered.

Joe nodded.

When they got to their seats, Elisabeth, Heather, and Alice were already there, but Joe noticed that Baron von Battenberg was conspicuously absent.

"Where's your father tonight?" Frank asked Elisabeth.

"Oh, he's around, just checking on the last-minute details," Elisabeth said. "Why?"

"We just wanted to compliment him on Aéro-cirque," Joe said. He motioned to the crowd. "I don't mean to sound crass, but this is bringing in a lot of money."

"Well, not as much as you might think," Elisabeth said. "The expenses are huge. Acrobats, helicopters, pilots, stadium fees, insurance." She shook her head. "He'll be lucky if he breaks even."

Elisabeth suddenly looked away as if she was

thinking of something else, so neither Frank nor Joe continued the discussion.

After several minutes of chitchat with Heather and Alice—who Frank thought must be great actresses considering that they didn't really want to be with Elisabeth—the public address system crackled. An announcer said, "We wish to apologize, but High-Wire Troupe D will not be performing tonight."

Joe felt as though somebody had slugged him. He looked over at Frank and nodded.

"Heather and Alice gave me and Joe a tour of historic Philadelphia this afternoon," Frank said, "and just as we were leaving, we thought we saw you."

Elisabeth blinked, gave Heather and Alice a funny look, then turned back to Frank. "Well, yes, I was doing the same thing for some of the acrobats," she said. "They're interested in American history too."

"High-Wire Troupe D?" Joe asked.

It was clear to Frank that Elisabeth was getting uncomfortable.

"Well, as a matter of fact, yes, and it's probably all my fault that they're not here tonight, because I insisted they have one of our famous Philly cheese steak sandwiches," Elisabeth said, "The place where we went was, well . . . kind of a greasy spoon. Their stomachs probably aren't used to that."

Frank looked down the aisle and saw Mario headed in their direction. He stood up. "I just thought of something that Joe and I need to talk to Mario about," he said. He turned to Heather and Alice. "Could you make sure these three," he pointed to Chet, Matt, and Tony, "get back to the Zettarella's?"

"Of course," Alice said.

"It'll be our pleasure!" Heather added.

"Where are you going?" Elisabeth asked.

Joe could hear the concern in her voice. "I hope we're going to solve a mystery," he said.

The Hardy boys hurried down the aisle to intercept Mario.

When they reached him, Joe said, "We need to head downtown!"

"Why? What's wrong?" Mario said.

"High-Wire Troupe D isn't performing tonight," Frank said. "That's the troupe Elisabeth was with downtown this afternoon."

"They weren't looking at the historic sights," Joe said. "Frank and I think they were casing some of the high-rise apartment buildings."

"*What?*" Mario said.

"We'll tell you all about it on the way downtown," Frank said.

The three of them raced toward gate forty-two. Mario radioed the police officer he had talked to earlier and told him to have the van running.

Within minutes, they were out of the stadium parking lot and heading back downtown. The traffic was heavier tonight, but Mario expertly maneuvered the van through it all.

When they finally reached downtown, Mario said, "Do you remember exactly where you were when you saw the acrobats looking up at the high-rise apartments?"

"I think so," Frank said.

"Wasn't it just past Benjamin Franklin's grave?" Joe said.

"Yes, it was, Joe—you're right," Frank said. "Hurry—we don't have much time!"

Mario made a couple of turns, drove back north for several blocks, then said, "Does this look familiar?"

Frank and Joe stuck their heads out the van's windows and scanned the skyline.

"Over there!" Joe said. "I'm sure of it."

"I think he's right, Mario," Frank agreed. "Let's head down that street."

Mario made a U-turn and headed toward a couple of high-rise apartment buildings that were across the street from each other. A half block away, he parked the van and the three of them got out.

"Do you have any binoculars?" Joe asked.

"As a matter of fact, I do," Mario said. "Did you see something suspicious?"

"Not yet," Joe said.

Mario handed him the binoculars, and Joe looked at the top apartments on the high-rise to his left.

"Joe! Wrong one!" Frank said. "I think there's something hanging from the railing of one of those balconies on the other apartment building!"

Joe moved the binoculars toward where Frank was pointing. "You're right!" he said. "Here, Mario, take a look!"

Mario adjusted the binoculars and looked. "I see a grappling hook. There's a long rope dangling from it." Mario handed the binoculars back to Joe. "Count the floors. I'm calling for backup. If we're lucky, we've got a robbery in progress."

After Mario was off the phone, he said, "I don't want to wait. I'll need your help, boys, but I want you to stay behind me until I know exactly what's happening, okay?"

"Okay," Frank said. "We've done this before—we understand."

With Mario leading the way, they raced toward the entrance to the apartment building. Mario showed the doorman his identification.

"I think there's a robbery taking place on the forty-seventh floor," he said. "We need to—"

"Impossible," the doorman said, interrupting and moving to block their way. "This building has the best security in the city, and there's no way—"

This time Mario interrupted with, "If you don't move right now and show me the elevator to the forty-seventh floor, then I'll take you downtown and bust you for impeding this investigation."

"Yes, sir," the doorman said, "but I honestly—"

"Show us the elevator!" Mario shouted.

When they reached the bank of elevators that would take them to the forty-seventh floor, Mario said, "Do these elevators open into the foyers of the apartments?"

"No, sir," the doorman said. "They open into hallways. There are four apartments on each floor."

"Are any of the tenants inside their apartments on that floor?" Mario asked.

"No, sir," the doorman said. "They're all at the Aérocirque show."

Joe nodded at Frank. "That figures," he said.

"Let me have your pass key," Mario said.

The doorman reluctantly handed it to him. "I'm only supposed to use this in an emergency," he said.

"This *is* an emergency," Frank said.

"In just a few minutes, this place is going to be covered with police officers," Mario said, "so you need to be prepared."

"Yes, sir," the doorman said.

The elevator arrived in seconds, and soon Mario, Frank, and Joe were on the forty-seventh floor. They carefully stepped out into the corridor.

"There are two apartments on each side of the

building," Mario said. "The rope was dangling from the balcony of one of the apartments on the street side."

"That means it's either 4701 or 4702," Joe said.

"Let's try 4701 first, but we need to be very careful," Mario said. "Make sure you guys stay behind me."

Using the pass key, Mario slowly opened the door to 4701. "Police!" he shouted. "Stay where you are!"

After they had waited in silence for several seconds, Joe said, "It looks like it's 4702."

The plush carpet of the corridor masked their footsteps as they hurried toward the next apartment.

Mario inserted the pass key and slowly opened the door. There was no one in the second apartment either.

"I have a feeling that the rope dangling from the balcony means the thieves had to leave in a hurry," Frank said.

Joe nodded. "Which means that somebody tipped them off that we were coming," he said.

9 Undercover!

As Mario, Frank, and Joe headed toward the balcony, Mario said, "Would you care to venture a guess as to who's behind this?"

"I have a feeling it's all connected to some of the acrobats in Aérocirque," Frank said.

"Maybe it's not just *some* of them, Frank," Joe said. "It could be *all* of them."

"I think I agree with Joe, Frank," Mario said.

"That would be a major crime operation, but I guess it would make sense, given that each night there's a troupe of acrobats that don't perform," Frank said.

"Well, we know now that we were right about what made all those scratches on the balconies,"

Joe said. "That grappling hook and that rope are pretty much a dead giveaway."

Mario nodded. "The evidence technicians will check everything out," he said, "but I doubt if there's anything here that will tie Aérocirque to the robberies."

"While we're waiting for them, let me tell you about another one of my theories," Frank said. He pointed to the apartment building across the street. "I think that somehow the thieves shoot the rope from the top of an apartment building across the street and tightrope walk to the empty apartment."

"That's a little far-fetched, isn't it, Frank?" Mario said. "Wouldn't people see them?"

"Think about it, Mario. Who goes around looking up in the sky all the time?" Frank said. "People are so busy hurrying to wherever it is they're going that they seldom look *around,* much less *up.* Anyway, the thieves do it at night. That makes it less likely they'll be seen."

"Frank's theory makes a lot of sense, Mario," Joe said.

"Well, I guess that means you still believe they reached the top of the other apartment building by helicopter," Mario said.

"Maybe not the apartment building itself, but a building nearby," Frank said. "Just look around you. There are helicopters flying all over the night skies of Philadelphia. Police. Radio and television personnel. Doctors. People don't pay attention anymore."

"If they happen to hear a helicopter that's a little louder than usual, they probably just think something's going on nearby," Joe added. "Unfortunately, people don't want to get involved in anything that doesn't immediately concern them anymore, so they ignore it."

"Why don't they land on top of the apartment building?" Mario asked.

"Maybe they don't want to take a chance on the *one* person in the apartment building who would get curious about the noise," Frank said. "They land on office buildings, where there are fewer people around at night."

Just then some midtown detectives arrived, along with the evidence technicians.

Frank and Joe followed Mario back into the living room. "It's all yours, guys. I can almost assure you that you won't find anything inside the apartment," Mario said, "but there's a grappling hook and a rope attached to it out on the balcony, which I want to see if you can connect to Aérocirque."

"That flying circus that's in town?" one of the evidence technicians said. "You're kidding me."

"No, I'm not," Mario said. "Come on, boys," he said to Frank and Joe. "We have some plans to make."

When they reached the lobby they passed the owner of the apartment, who was demanding that the police let him and his wife in immediately.

"It won't be long, sir," one of the officers was saying. "It's important that we look for evidence to help solve this crime spree."

The front doors closed on Frank and Joe before they could hear what the apartment owner said.

After they climbed back into the van and started heading out of downtown Philadelphia toward Mario's house, he said, "I have an idea. It could be dangerous, but my officers and I will be with you all the way, and I think it's the only way we're going to catch these guys."

"Let's hear it," Joe said. "We've been in dangerous situations before."

"Yeah, it's nothing new," Frank agreed.

"Tomorrow night is Aérocirque's last performance," Mario said. "There's only one troupe that has performed every night: the Masked High-Wire Troupe. Something tells me they'll be the ones to rob an apartment building tomorrow night."

"Oh, yeah!" Frank said. "They're the guys who never take off their masks when they're around the other acrobats."

"Right. They belong to some sort of cult that makes them use masks," Mario said. "None of the other acrobats have ever seen their faces."

"Where do we fit in?" Joe asked.

"Well, every troupe is at the stadium until right before the circus begins," Mario said. "The one troupe that doesn't perform leaves just after it's announced that someone has taken ill."

Frank and Joe nodded.

"So, if my officers and I can slip you boys into the troupe as they're leaving, then you can be in on the robbery," Mario said. "We'll have you wired, so we'll know where you are every minute."

"You expect us to walk one of the wires?" Joe asked.

Mario shook his head. "Absolutely not, Joe," he said. "Two of the acrobats are always the anchors during the performance. They never walk the wire."

"You're sure?" Frank said.

"I'm sure," Mario said. "They're there to help the walkers back onto the platform."

"So you think these two anchor acrobats stay on the roof of the building opposite the apartment being robbed, sort of like lookouts for the guys walking the rope?" Joe said.

Mario sighed. "I guess it does sound kind of far-fetched," he finally said. "Let's just forget it and see if we can think of a more sensible solution."

"No, Mario, this doesn't sound far-fetched at all," Frank said. "In fact, it sounds brilliant. And Joe and I could certainly handle the detective work required."

They were nearing Mario's neighborhood.

"I'm thinking that tomorrow morning—early— the three of us should head out to the stadium, where I'll make it known that it's very important to the Philadelphia Police Department that some important visitors practice with the masked troupe," Mario said. "They may not want it, but I don't think they'll say anything, because if they're really behind all these robberies, they won't want to irritate me."

"Sounds like a plan," Frank said. He turned to Joe. "We need to go to bed right when we get home," he added. "Circus performers need their sleep!"

The next morning, bright and early, before Chet, Matt, or Tony was awake, Mario took Frank and Joe to the stadium. When they arrived, all of the Aérocirque acrobats were unloading from two charter buses.

"I hadn't even thought about this," Joe said, "but where do they stay at night?"

"Baron von Battenberg has rented an entire motel just a couple of miles from here," Mario said.

"They're probably too smart to stash any of the stolen items there," Frank said.

"Probably," Mario agreed. "Of course, we're not sure they're behind these robberies," he added. "It could just be a coincidence. Somebody could be setting them up."

Joe shook his head. "The people behind these

high-rise apartment robberies are trained acrobats, Mario," he said, "and I'm assuming that the only trained acrobats in Philadelphia are the ones from Aérocirque."

Mario nodded.

"So we should proceed as planned," Frank said.

Mario pulled the police van up behind the last bus, and the three of them got out. They headed toward the smaller practice tent. "The Masked High-Wire Troupe is the only one that practices here," he said. "They're completely separate from the others."

"I just thought of something, Mario. This is the most acrobatic team in Aérocirque," Joe said. "I have a feeling that they're saving the best for last. Whoever they're going to rob tonight must be somebody really special."

"I guess we'll find out tonight," Mario whispered.

As they approached the entrance to the tent, Frank reviewed the plans he and Joe had made before they went to bed last night.

Mario would tell Baron von Battenberg that Frank and Joe were so enthralled by what they had seen in Aérocirque that they were planning a mini act at Bayport High School to raise money for charity. Of course, their circus wouldn't have helicopters, but it would have high-wire acts, and Frank and Joe wanted to train with some of the acrobats to learn what they could. Mario would tell Baron von Battenberg that the group Frank and Joe most admired was the masked troupe. If the baron refused to let the boys shadow that troupe, Mario had told them, he would explain that he wasn't above not only pulling their permit for tonight's performance in Philadelphia but contacting his network of police officer friends along Aérocirque's tour and suggesting they do the same thing. Mario assured the Hardy boys that the baron would come through.

As it turned out, Mario was right on the money. The baron didn't hesitate when Mario suggested that Frank and Joe practice with the masked troupe.

"Of course, you'll have to wear costumes and masks too," Baron von Battenberg told them. "The acrobats in this troupe never practice without their costumes and masks. They won't work with anyone who isn't wearing them."

"We were counting on that," Joe told him. "Weren't we, Frank?"

Frank smiled and nodded. "Yes, we were," he said.

The baron clapped his hands. One of the masked troupe members looked up and the baron motioned him over to where they were standing. Instead of speaking to the acrobat, he mimed that he wanted Frank and Joe to put on costumes and masks and practice with the troupe.

The acrobat nodded, then he motioned for Frank and Joe to follow them.

Joe followed, but Frank turned to the baron. "What language do they speak?" he asked.

"They don't," the baron replied. "They're all deaf."

Suddenly, Frank wondered if their plan was going to work. "Were you using sign language?" he asked.

The baron shook his head. "They don't know that, either," he replied. "They just act out what they want people to do, and that seems to work."

"So what you're saying is that none of them use the same signs to let the others know what they want?" Frank asked.

"That's about it," the baron said. "They're a peculiar lot, but they're the most exciting of the acrobats. They have nerves of steel. I think that comes with not being able to hear the crowd noise. Nothing throws them off."

Joe and the masked acrobat were now on the other side of the tent. They had stopped, and the acrobat was motioning for Frank to hurry.

"Thanks very much again," Frank said. He turned and started running toward them.

The acrobat showed the Hardy boys to the dressing room. He mimed that he would be by in a few minutes to pick them up.

Frank and Joe quickly found costumes and

masks exactly like the ones the rest of the masked troupe were wearing.

When they were dressed, the boys went outside the tent to the practice ring used by the masked troupe. The first acrobat had already communicated why Frank and Joe were there, and the Hardy boys were pleasantly surprised that all of the acrobats were willing to show them what they did on the high wire.

For the rest of the morning, Frank and Joe practiced their "act." They started just two feet off the ground, so that when they fell, they usually landed on their feet. Gradually, the wires were raised, and by the time the wires were ten feet high, the Hardy boys were almost gliding from platform to platform.

The anchors mimed that the Hardy boys should join their troupe. Frank and Joe did their best to tell them that they'd have to think about it.

At lunch the Hardy boys ate alone. Each member of the troupe went off by himself, possibly so they could remove their masks to eat without anyone seeing their faces.

During the afternoon Frank and Joe stayed on the platform, and the wires got higher and higher. Around four o'clock, when the day's practice concluded, the Hardy boys felt that they would be able to implement their plan.

Frank and Joe managed to slip away from the rest of the acrobats as they headed for the dressing room. They met Mario at the police van.

"We're set," Joe said. "We'll point out the two anchors to your men."

"If they can hold them until Joe and I have left in the helicopters with the rest of the team," Frank said, "we should be able to pull this off."

"Actually, I'm still wondering if this is a good idea," Mario said. "It's dangerous."

Joe shook his head. "Frank and I really got to know these guys today, Mario," he said. "We especially studied the mannerisms of the anchors, and since they don't talk to each other, there's nothing to give us away."

Frank nodded. "Don't worry, Mario," he said. "We can pull this off. Tonight, this crime spree will be over."

10 High-wire Act

Frank and Joe quickly jumped into the police van unobserved.

"What now?" Joe asked.

"We wait," Mario said. "One of my officers will radio me when they abduct the two anchors, and that'll be your signal to slip back into the tent to join the troupe."

Mario left the van running, which allowed cooler air to circulate. Because of the tinted windows, it was possible for the Hardy boys to move around inside, unnoticed by anyone who walked by.

"I need to put this wire on you, Frank," Mario said. He took a small black object out of a box. "The latest thing," he said.

"It looks like a light-switch plate," Joe said.

Mario nodded. "You wear it on your leg," he said. "It has an adhesive that sticks to the skin but pulls off easily."

"Good," Frank said. "I can't stand those bandages that hurt more coming off than what they were healing!"

"You won't feel a thing when this is removed," Mario said, "and there's very little chance that it'll be discovered."

"That's important," Joe said.

Mario nodded. "This will be our only communication with you," he said, "and you'll have to figure out a way to tell us where you are without the other acrobats seeing you."

Frank nodded. "They might wonder why we start talking to ourselves all of a sudden," he said. "The masks won't hide the movement of our mouths."

"Exactly," Mario said. "I have men stationed all along the routes downtown, so we should be able to keep the helicopter in sight, but once downtown, I don't want my officers to be so visible that we'll scare the acrobats off. It'll be up to you, Frank, to guide us to the right apartment building."

Suddenly, Mario's radio crackled. "I'm listening," he said.

Mario nodded, then added, "They're going in." To Frank and Joe, he said, "It's time." He opened the van door, stuck his head out, and pronounced the coast clear. Frank and Joe jumped out and quickly entered the tent.

Frank could see that the rest of the troupe was over near the opposite entrance. One of the masked acrobats saw them and motioned angrily for them to hurry up.

"Uh-oh, I hope we're not going to have to explain our absence in sign language," Joe whispered. "I'm not quite sure how far I can get."

Fortunately, they didn't have to worry. When they finally reached the rest of the masked troupe, Baron von Battenberg entered the tent, and all the acrobats turned their attention to him.

Just then, on the opposite side of the building, a speaker begin to play loud music.

Frank and Joe looked at each other. There was no way Mario would be able to pick up any of this conversation.

"The Philadelphia Arms is our target building," Baron von Battenberg said. "It opened last year and is home to some of the city's wealthiest residents."

One of the acrobats mimed something to the baron which Frank didn't understand, but which the baron obviously did.

"There will only be four of you tonight, Piet," the baron said. "You and Serge and the two anchors."

The Hardy boys looked at each other. These mimes must be able to read lips.

Another acrobat mimed a question which Joe thought he understood.

"I've decided that we're not going to cancel any of the acts tonight, because I think the police are getting suspicious," Baron von Battenberg said. "No one will notice that four of you are gone. The rest of the troupe will take up the slack, I'm sure."

The acrobats all nodded.

"Good," Baron von Battenberg said.

Joe shot Frank a quick glance. He was actually stunned that they had been right all along about who the crooks were.

Frank breathed a sigh of relief when Piet and Serge motioned for the Hardy boys to follow them. *It's working!* he thought. *They think we're the regular anchors!*

Just outside the entrance to the tent, a black helicopter was waiting for them. They all bent over to avoid the whirling blades and quickly ran for the chopper.

At the door, Piet and Serge stopped so Frank and Joe could get into the back seat, then the two acrobats climbed in after them.

"Good! We won't be the first ones out," Joe whispered to Frank. "As long as we just do whatever Piet and Serge do, we should be okay."

"I hope you're right," Frank said.

The helicopter lifted off and headed toward downtown Philadelphia.

Frank was astounded at how noisy it was inside the helicopter. Once again, he was sure that Mario wouldn't be able to hear anything he tried to tell him. He'd just have to wait until they landed to check in.

Out one of the small rear windows, Frank thought he recognized some of the landmarks he remembered seeing when they were driving back and forth with Mario. He was sure they were following Highway 611 toward downtown Philadelphia. That was good, he knew, since Mario had his officers stationed along the route.

Frank only hoped they knew which helicopter the Hardy boys were in. Just in the few minutes they had been in the air, Frank had already counted six other helicopters crowding the night sky. *It's clear why nobody would be suspicious of a helicopter flying over their apartment building,* Frank thought. *Most people have probably tuned them out.*

Up ahead through the front windshield Joe could see the skyscrapers of downtown Philadelphia. He thought he recognized the two apartment buildings that had already been burgled. He didn't know which one of the remaining buildings was the Philadelphia Arms. Joe knew that many American cities had worked hard to revitalize their downtown areas, and that bringing people back there to live was a major part of what city leaders hoped to accomplish. If he and Frank could do their part to help put an end to these high-rise burglaries, then that migration would continue.

Frank leaned forward. They had reached the first skyscraper at the edge of the city's downtown area, and the pilot slowed down. As they passed over the other buildings, it seemed they were only a few feet from their tops. Frank was sure they'd be landing soon.

Below, Joe could see some of the historical landmarks they had visited the day before. He shook his head in amazement. When they had taken their tour of Philadelphia's historical district, he remembered looking up once and seeing a police helicopter flying over. Little did he know that within twenty-four hours, he himself would be in a helicopter with a couple of acrobatic criminals flying over the same area.

Suddenly, the helicopter wasn't moving but was instead hovering just a few feet over a building.

Frank nudged Joe. "This is the one," he whispered. "From here on out, we have to play everything by ear."

"I know," Joe whispered back. "Be careful."

"You be careful too," Frank whispered.

The pilot signaled that he was lowering ropes.

Out his side window, Frank saw a rope fall. He looked over and saw Joe peering out his window. Frank was sure that another rope was being lowered on that side too.

Serge turned and motioned for Frank to follow his lead. Piet did the same to Joe.

Within seconds, Serge was out of the helicopter and sliding down the rope. Frank was right behind him. He now knew the reason why all of the masked acrobats also wore heavy gloves. Even with them on, he could feel the heat of the friction.

As Joe slid down the rope on his side, he saw Frank reach the end of the other rope and jump the few remaining feet. He did the same, but as he landed, he saw Piet lying on the roof, holding his ankle. Joe didn't know what to do now. It was obvious that Piet was in a lot of pain.

Serge hurried over to Piet, but Frank stayed where he was a few feet away. *What's he doing?* Joe wondered. He wanted to find out, but he was sure that might make Serge suspicious. He stayed where he was, so that if Serge mimed for him to help with Piet, he'd be right there.

Above them, the helicopter was flying away into the night sky. Serge looked up at Joe and mimed that he needed help to carry Piet across the roof. Quickly, Joe made himself available. He grabbed

Piet under one arm, and Serge grabbed him under the other.

As they propped Piet up against a wall, Joe glanced over and saw that Frank's back was to them. He hoped that his brother was trying to reach Mario and tell him where they were so that he and his officers would be able to catch the acrobats in the act of robbing the apartment.

Serge did what he could to make Piet comfortable, then looked around for Frank. Joe was glad that Frank had evidently finished with his directions and was walking toward them.

At first Frank had been grateful for what had happened to Piet, but when he landed he'd felt the wire jar loose and fall through his pants to the roof. The adhesive hadn't held. In the darkness he couldn't see where it had landed, and he knew he could only spend so much time looking for it or Serge would get suspicious. *Now how will Mario know where we are?* he wondered. How would this affect the operation?

Just as Frank reached them, Serge mimed that he wanted Joe to go pick up a black bag that lay where Piet had fallen.

Joe remembered seeing it when he landed, but it hadn't registered that it was something that Piet had been carrying. He hurried across the roof, picked up the black canvas bag—which was heavier than it looked—then took it back over to Serge.

Serge opened the bag, felt around, then nodded that everything was okay.

Good, Joe thought. It was important that the operation not be abandoned.

Frank felt the same way, but somehow he had to figure out a way to contact Mario. He wasn't exactly sure what was in the black bag, but he was sure it had something to do with how the acrobats made it across to the apartment being robbed. With Piet out of commission, that meant that Serge would be the only one to do the job, but that would still work. Even if Mario and his officers only caught *one* thief in the act, that would be enough, especially since Serge would probably implicate the others. Piet was in no condition to do anything to them, Frank decided, even if he and Joe contacted Mario in front of him.

Serge picked up the black canvas bag and motioned for Frank and Joe to follow him to the edge of the roof.

When they got there, Serge pointed to a balcony across the street, mimed that that was the apartment they were going to rob, then opened the canvas bag.

The Hardy boys were stunned by what happened next.

Serge pulled out what looked liked a small shoulder-held missile launcher. He quickly aimed it toward the balcony, pushed a button, and with a *whoosh* sound, a grappling hook and rope shot across to the target. The hook grabbed the metal railing and held fast.

Next, Serge attached the launcher to a metal pipe coming from the roof. He pushed another button and the rope tightened.

What happened next stunned the Hardy Boys. Serge mimed that it was Frank and Joe who were going to walk the wire.

Frank mimed that he and Joe were anchors and that Serge should walk the wire. Serge shook his head.

Joe thought quickly. With all the training they had gotten yesterday, he thought that he and Frank could do it, but just the thought that this rope was now probably fifty or more stories off the ground—instead of just a few feet—sent chills through him. But he had little choice. He mimed to Serge that they would do it.

Frank had already decided that there was no way out, so he was glad that Joe was okay with it. If they were going to catch these crooks, they couldn't abandon the operation now. Thanks to years of training by their father, he and Joe both had nerves of steel when it came to things like this, so he was sure they could pull it off. In fact, a plan was already beginning to form in his head. When they reached the apartment, they'd call Mario.

Serge handed Joe a piece of paper and a small

red clip. There was enough light on the top of the building that Joe could tell that the paper showed how to disarm the apartment's security system. From what Joe could tell, there was a small circuitry box on the balcony doors. All they had to do was attach the red clip, and that would somehow confuse the system. Joe was amazed at how high-tech this operation was.

Serge motioned for them to hurry.

Frank looked at Joe, nodded, then stepped out onto the high-wire. Joe was right behind him. Slowly, they felt their way. There was no wind tonight, for which they were thankful. One of the real acrobats might have been able to adjust to that, but neither Frank nor Joe was sure they could have.

When he was a few feet from the edge of the building, Frank felt a sense of euphoria. He had grown up with the belief that he and his brother could accomplish anything they attempted, and he had to agree that walking a high-wire from one sky-scraper to another in downtown Philadelphia at night was one of the most daring things he had ever done. What also pushed him along was the thought that once they reached the balcony, disarmed the security system, and entered the apartment, he could use the telephone there to call Mario.

When Frank finally reached the balcony, he jumped off the rope onto the deck. Joe was right behind him. Frank told Joe about losing the radio.

"I knew you had lost something," Joe said. He took a deep breath. "Well, we're here, and I'm ready for this operation to end, so let's override this security system and call Mario."

"Sounds like a plan to me," Frank agreed.

They headed toward the doors that would take them into the apartment.

Suddenly, Joe stopped. "Uh-oh, we've got problems," he said.

"What's wrong?" Frank asked.

Joe showed him the sheet of paper that Serge had given him. "This plan is for a different security system, Frank," Joe said. He looked closely at the small label on the door. "The owners installed a new security system today!"

"That means if we try to break in, an alarm will sound, and we'll be caught," Frank said.

"Exactly," Joe said. "Serge and Piet will see what's happening, and they'll escape. If they're not on the roof for Mario and his officers to find, it'll just be our word against theirs, and we'll be back where we started."

Just then Frank looked up to see Mario's face staring at him through the French doors.

11 A Change of Plans

Quickly, Mario unlocked the French doors, and the Hardy boys slipped inside the dark apartment removing their masks.

Joe could barely make out Bill and some other uniformed officers just beyond him.

"Are you boys all right?" Mario said.

Frank thought it was strange that Mario hadn't asked why he and Joe were on the balcony instead of the other acrobats, but he nodded, then explained everything that had happened since they left the stadium. "But how did you know where to find us? It was so noisy in the helicopter that I thought it would be impossible for you to hear anything I said, and then when we jumped onto the roof, I lost the radio, and I never did locate it."

"My officers on the ground had you in sight all the way," Mario said.

"Well, we're glad you're here," Joe said.

But Frank wasn't so sure. Something wasn't adding up.

"The alarm system isn't the one on the piece of paper Serge gave us," Joe said. "We knew that if we tried to break in, an alarm would sound."

"We didn't want that to happen," Frank added, "because we were sure it would alert Serge and Piet, and they'd escape."

Mario nodded. "Good thinking," he said.

"What now?" Bill asked Mario.

Mario looked at Frank and Joe. "Uh, were you planning to walk the rope back across and tell the acrobats what the problem was?" he said.

"Well, that's what we were planning to do before you showed up," Joe said, "but I'm not quite sure I like the idea of tempting fate a second time."

"I can understand that, I really can, boys," Mario said, "but would you be willing to do it to help bring this case to a close?"

Frank looked over at Joe. "This isn't the first dangerous situation we've ever been in, so let's do it," he said. He turned back to Mario. "We're committed to solving this case, so we'll do whatever is necessary to catch the thieves."

"They may not believe you," Mario said.

"We're prepared for that," Frank said. "In my

head I'm already trying to figure out how to mime our story."

"I just thought of something," Joe said. "We never did talk about what happens after they've robbed the apartment."

"They probably hoist the loot in a helicopter," Frank said.

"That makes sense," Joe said.

"What's the plan now, Mario?" Frank asked. "Serge and Piet aren't doing anything on that roof except maybe trespassing, so how are we going to work this?"

"If you can take your time walking the rope, that'll give me and my officers enough lead time to make it over to the roof of that building," Mario said.

"I have a night vision camera in the van. If we can get pictures of you two miming the break-in, with reactions from the acrobats," Bill said, "then that, along with your testimony, might be enough to get a conviction."

Mario looked at Frank and Joe. "It's weak, I know, but at the moment, since we're dealing with the troupe that can't talk, it's about all we can do."

"Okay. We'll do our best," Joe said.

Frank nodded. "We'll make sure that what they mime will look to a jury like they're talking about breaking into an apartment."

With Joe in the lead, the Hardy boys left the dark

apartment and headed back to where the grappling hook was attached to the metal railing.

"I'm really impressed at how easily Mario and his officers found just the right apartment, Joe," Frank said. "They're either really good or really lucky."

"I know," Joe said. He looked over toward the roof. "I don't see either Serge or Piet, but maybe they're just in the shadows. Anyway, they probably wouldn't be hanging over the sides of the building while we were robbing the apartment, because people might notice them."

"Right," Frank said. "They probably have a pretty good idea of how long this takes, and they could just be resting until they think it's time for us to come back."

Joe looked over at his brother. "I just thought of something else, Frank," he said. "How are we going to get off that roof?"

"Well, I really do think that loose rope hanging from the balcony yesterday was just a backup plan," Frank said. He scanned the skies. "I'd say they normally escape the same way they arrived, by helicopter, although I don't see one hovering around. It probably hasn't been long enough."

"Well, I'm going to start miming my story now," Joe said. He leaned over the railing and started shrugging, to indicate that there was a problem and that he and Frank didn't know what to do.

Frank joined him. He mimed trying to break into the apartment, suddenly stopping and covering his ears to keep from hearing a loud alarm.

"I think we've killed all the time we can, so I guess we should start across," Joe said. He put one foot on the metal railing, then lifted the rest of his body until both feet were together. Slowly, he began to stand up. He tentatively put one foot on the rope, and felt its tension. "It's still tight. We can do this."

Inch by inch, Joe made his way along the rope and away from the edge of the apartment building. *This is totally nuts!* he thought.

Behind him, Frank waited until Joe was several feet away and over the street before he got on the rope. *If I make it across,* Frank thought, *I never want to see another high-wire act!*

Frank had just reached the edge of the building when he thought he saw Mario getting into a car below. Neither Bill nor any of the other officers were in sight. *They must have parked in a less conspicuous spot than the front of the building,* Frank thought. That made sense. They were probably going to take a roundabout way to reach the building he and Joe were now heading to. Frank hoped they reached it in time. He didn't know how long they could mime to Serge and Piet what happened without the helicopter returning to take them away—*if* that was how they escaped.

Joe knew that Frank was behind him, but he was concentrating on maintaining his balance. On the walk over he had been relaxed, because he knew that all he and Joe had to do was to make sure that Mario and his officers would be waiting for them. But now Joe was wondering what lay ahead. Suddenly his concentration was broken by the sound of sirens in the street below. Joe stopped walking. Slowly, he looked down. Several vehicles with flashing lights were racing past.

Frank stopped walking within seconds after Joe had. He also looked down to see what was happening. The vehicles were now close enough that he recognized two fire engines, three ambulances, and five squad cars. *This doesn't look good,* he thought. When the vehicles stopped in front of the building they were heading toward, Frank decided it looked even worse.

Joe made a quick decision. Even though they were closer to the building they had just come from, they had to do what they could to stop the Aérocirque crime spree. He resumed walking toward where he hoped Serge and Piet were waiting. Joe could only hope that the confusion on the street wouldn't delay Mario and his officers. If he and Frank hurried, they might get to the acrobats in time, mime their story, and trust that Mario would get it on film.

Way to go, Joe, Frank thought as he watched Joe

pick up his pace across the rope. If they were going to bring everyone associated with this crime spree to justice, there was no turning back.

Just then a police helicopter swooped dangerously close to the Hardy boys, causing enough air turbulence that both Frank and Joe lost their balance.

Joe managed to fall on his seat, where he balanced for a couple of seconds, then straddled the rope—but Frank was frantically hanging on by his hands.

"Frank!" Joe called when he saw the precarious situation his brother was in. "Let me help!"

"No, no! I'm okay!" Frank shouted. "If you can't stand up, then just slide along to the edge of the building. I've got enough grip with these gloves that I can manage to swing my way there."

Quickly, Joe pulled himself toward the other building. It was actually not as difficult to balance this way as it was walking.

Frank's only concern was that when he started swinging toward the building, it would unbalance his brother—so he just hung by his hands until he decided Joe was far enough along that there would be no problem. Frank was thankful for all of the hours of gymnastics practice. His arms were strong, so he knew he could make it. When he looked up once, he saw that Joe had reached the edge of the building. And he was happy to see that Serge was there to lend him a helping hand.

Just a few more feet, Frank thought, *and then we'll go into our act. We'll make sure that whatever Serge mimes, it'll be easy to tell that we were all here tonight to rob that apartment.*

12 Prisoners

Now Joe could see Serge and Piet. It was as if they had suddenly appeared out of nowhere. Both of them were standing together at the edge of the roof with their hands outstretched. Below him, the activity in the street seemed to be picking up. Joe wasn't sure if it was that or if something else was making him nervous, but he was glad that he only had a few more feet to go before he was safely across the rope.

Something's not right, Frank thought as he watched Joe nearing the end of the rope. It was just a feeling, but he had had this feeling before, and he knew to trust his instincts.

Just then another helicopter swooped by. It all happened so fast that Frank didn't get a good look at it; it was all he could do to hang on to the rope. Still, he had seen enough of it in his peripheral vision to know that it wasn't a police helicopter. Frank felt a prickling on his skin. If it was the Aéro-cirque helicopter, he and Joe would really have to work fast to make sure they gave Mario and his officers what they needed before they swooped in and arrested the two acrobats.

Up ahead, Joe had reached the end of the rope and was taking Serge's hand, but then Frank saw something he couldn't quite understand. Serge seemed to jerk Joe off the rope, and within seconds all three had disappeared from sight. *Did something happen on the roof?* Frank wondered. Had one of the acrobats spotted Mario and his officers? Had they pulled Joe down for his protection?

Slowly, Frank slid his hands along the rope. Now another helicopter swooped overhead—or was it the one he had just seen? Frank had always prided himself on being able to stay focused, but now, with the wind disturbance the helicopter had created, the confusion on the street below, and his wondering what was actually happening on the roof, Frank felt himself starting to spiral out of control. He stopped for a split second, just long enough to take two quick deep breaths to calm himself, then he began sliding his hands along the rope again. Unlike their first walk, on their way to the apartment, the trip back seemed endless. If the rope had been covered in tar, Frank decided, it would have been easier to maneuver.

Soon Frank was only inches from the end of the rope. Suddenly, Serge rose before him. His hand was stretched out toward Frank.

"Hurry, Frank," Serge said. "We don't have much time."

Frank grabbed Serge's hand. "I'm hurrying. It's kind of—"

Two things happened simultaneously. Frank realized that Serge was talking just as Serge yanked him off the rope. He landed with a thud on the graveled roof of the building. When Frank tried to move, Serge's powerful foot kept him pinned down.

"You can talk," Frank managed to say.

"Of course we can talk," Piet said. Frank hadn't seen the man, but he knew from the direction of his voice that he was just a few feet away. "You don't really think the baron went around Europe looking for acrobats who were hearing and speech impaired, do you? It was just part of the act—and it worked, too."

"Where's my brother?" Frank demanded.

"I'm here, Frank," Joe said.

"Yes, yes, we're all here now," Serge said, "and in a few minutes, we're all going to be gone once again."

Frank was sure Serge was talking about the heli-copter. Somehow he had to find out from Joe if

Mario and his officers were anywhere nearby.

"Okay, okay, so we didn't fool you," Frank said. He tried to sit up, but once again, Serge's powerful foot shoved him back to the roof. The tiny pieces of gravel felt sharp against his skin. "We just wanted to be a part of the circus. We didn't mean any harm. At school, we're members of the gymnastics team, and we thought we'd be big men on campus if we actually walked the ropes with you guys. We had no idea you were into this. If you'll just let us go, we won't talk."

"Oh, so the great Hardy boys won't talk if we let them go," Serge said with a snarl. "We're not stupid."

"They know all about us, Frank," Joe said.

"Your brother's right, Frank," Piet said. "We know all about you."

"What do you know?" Frank said.

Serge grinned menacingly. "Oh, you'll find out soon enough," he said, "and I think you'll be really surprised, too."

"You'll never get away with this," Joe said. "The Philadelphia police know where you are."

"Of course they do," Serge said, "but they'll never make it to the roof in time. The baron's friends won't let them. We're masters at creating diversions, and you're witnessing one of the biggest diversions we've ever pulled off."

Who are the baron's 'friends'? Joe thought.

"What do you mean?" Frank asked.

"When the baron and his friends found out that things hadn't gone according to plan, he told us to put a few smoke bombs in strategic places while you were in the apartment across the street," Serge said. "This entire building has been shut down. If you're expecting the Philadelphia police department to rescue you in time, then you're out of luck."

"Serge is right," Piet said. He gave a laugh that chilled Joe to the bone. "We've got big plans for the Hardy boys."

A noise across the roof made Serge take his foot off Frank's back.

"Do you see the helicopter, Piet?" Serge called.

"No," Piet said.

"Well, it was here once, but the police helicopters must have radioed the pilot to stay clear of the building," Serge said. "He's probably waiting until he can slip in unnoticed from a different direction."

"I wish he'd hurry up," Piet said. "This is taking too long." He quickly wiped his brow.

Suddenly Joe had hope. He had seen a crack in Piet's act. Underneath, the man was scared. Joe could use that against him.

"You'll never get off this roof alive, Piet," Joe whispered to him.

"Stop talking now," Piet whispered back. "You're the one who needs to worry."

"What's going on over there?" Serge called from the edge of the roof.

"Nothing," Piet shouted back.

Good—it's working, Joe thought. Piet could just as easily have told Serge what he had said, but the fact that he chose not to meant he was leaving his options open. He was keeping secrets. If Joe could put more chinks in the man's armor, he might be able to save himself and Frank.

Frank suddenly heard the noise of banging on metal. It sounded as though it was coming from the door that allowed access to the roof. He needed to signal Joe that it was time for action. "Well, Joe, I guess these guys have beaten us after all," he shouted. "We should have been smarter than to think we could outwit them."

Across the roof, Joe heard Frank's words loud and clear, and he knew exactly what they meant. They had used them many times before to disarm their captors and to take them off guard for just enough time so the Hardy boys could act.

"You're right, Frank," Joe shouted back. "What were we thinking?"

"You weren't thinking," Serge said. "That's the problem."

"No, here's the problem," Frank said as he grabbed hold of Serge's legs and pulled him down to the roof.

At the same time, Joe grabbed Piet from behind and pinned him against one of the air conditioning ducts. Piet was initially taken by surprise, so Joe had the upper hand for the first few minutes of the struggle, but soon Piet's superior strength began to make the difference. Still, Joe thought, if he could just keep Piet down long enough for Mario and his men to break down the door to the roof, he'd win.

Frank had Serge in a headlock, and the two of them were rolling around on the roof. Frank tried to keep his face free of the sharp rocks, but he felt as though all of the skin was being scraped off his hands and his arms.

Joe had his back pressed against Piet to pin him to the air conditioning duct. His heels were anchored against a metal pipe, and he was pushing with all his might, but he was quickly losing the battle. The banging against the roof door was getting louder, and Joe was just sure that Mario and his officers would break through any minute. If he could just hold on a little longer. . . .

Suddenly Frank saw the helicopter slowly descending toward the roof. As the wind from the blades began whipping up the small rocks on the roof, one struck him in the eye, causing a natural reflex to cover it with his hand. Just as he did, Serge took advantage to gain the upper hand. He managed to yank Frank up and get one of his powerful arms around Frank's neck. Frank tried to struggle, but it was useless, and his left eye was gushing tears.

The pilot lowered a rope from the hovering craft, and Serge tied it under Frank's arms. He gave the pilot the signal to pull Frank into the craft.

Joe watched as his brother was slowly pulled into the hovering helicopter. With Serge now free to help Piet, Joe knew that all was lost. "Okay, okay," he said. He quickly stood up and raised his hands. Joe could still hear the banging on the roof door, but he knew now that he and Frank would be long gone when Mario and his officers finally broke through.

13 Betrayed!

Joe was right. As he was being pulled into the helicopter, the metal door to the roof burst open, and Mario and his officers charged through. But they were too late. The pilot of the helicopter banked sharply, and they were instantly heading away.

Serge shoved Joe down between the rear seats where Frank was already lying. "Don't try anything else," he said. "If you do, I'm going to push you out."

"Just a couple of minutes more, and Mario would have made it," Frank managed to whisper to his brother. "We had them, Joe, but when the wind from the helicopter blades whipped up those pebbles, it was like buckshot on my skin."

"I know," Joe whispered back. "I wonder where they're taking us."

"I hope it's back to the stadium," Frank said. "At least we might have a chance if they do."

"I don't think that's going to happen, Frank," Joe whispered. "I'm glad they didn't have time to do that to me," he said, looking at the way Frank was tied. "They had to get me into the helicopter and get off the roof."

That might be the only advantage they had, Joe thought. If there were some way he could shift his weight enough, then he could untie Frank. Serge and Piet were having a heated conversation with the pilot. They weren't paying attention to Frank and Joe.

Perfect, Joe thought. Before he would be able to do anything, though, he needed to shift his body so he could get some circulation back into his arms. He brought his legs up against his stomach until he was able to use them as a lever to turn his torso. He could feel the blood slowly returning to his extremities.

"What's going on back there?" Serge demanded. He was leaning over his seat, looking at the Hardy boys.

"Nothing. One of my feet was asleep. I just moved it, that's all," Joe said. He suddenly decided he'd try something. "I want to sit up."

"Then sit up," Serge said.

Frank thought he detected disgust in the man's voice. Something had happened in the last few minutes, he was sure. He wondered if it had to do with the conversation that he and the pilot had just had.

Joe struggled to right himself, and was finally able to grab the back of his seat and pull himself into it. The rope used to pull him into the helicopter was still around his waist, so he undid it and tossed it behind his seat. He hadn't expected any help from either Serge or Piet, but he had to admit that he was puzzled when he realized they weren't watching him. It was almost as if they didn't care about the Hardy boys any longer.

Now that Joe was free, he set about untying Frank. Serge had done more than just tie the rope around Frank's waist so he could be pulled into the helicopter. Frank's feet and hands were tied too. Still, Joe managed to free his brother by working carefully with the knots.

Finally, both Hardy boys were upright in their seats and ready to find out their fate.

Frank was sure he could see boat traffic below. They were over water. Where were they headed? Just then Joe felt the helicopter bank, and he knew they were starting to descend. Within minutes, they had landed.

"We're going to get in that panel truck over there," Serge said. "Don't try anything. If it hadn't been for the baron's daughter, you'd already be at the bottom of the Atlantic."

Frank shuddered. He realized now that they had actually flown out of Philadelphia, across New

Jersey, and over the Atlantic, but that evidently Elisabeth had radioed the pilot at the last minute to bring the Hardy boys back. He couldn't imagine why, but he was glad. He was sure that Serge and Piet would have enjoyed shoving them out of the helicopter into the ocean below.

"I've already untied my brother," Joe said brazenly. "I thought that would make it faster for us after we landed." Serge gave him a funny look but didn't say anything.

The Hardy boys followed Serge and Piet out of the helicopter and then ran, bent over to avoid the whirling blades, toward the panel truck.

There were a couple of men waiting for them in the back, but they said nothing as Serge and Piet and the Hardy boys jumped inside. When they were all in, one of the men shut the sliding door, and they were enveloped in total darkness.

The panel truck sped away, leaving Frank to wonder where in the world they were headed. They had escaped a watery death by moments, so he didn't believe they had been saved only to die some other way, but with criminals like the Aéro-cirque gang, no one could be sure of anything.

Joe could tell from the speed and from the way the panel truck was riding that they were now on an expressway. Where they were headed, though, he could only guess.

Frank figured they had been in the panel truck

for about thirty minutes when they exited the expressway, stopped, then slowly made their way along surface streets. Then the vehicle dipped down as though they were headed into a tunnel of some kind. Once again he had a strange feeling in his stomach, as though maybe they had been saved from the ocean only to be subjected to something even more horrendous.

Joe had just shifted a little so he could lean over and whisper to Frank when the panel truck finally stopped. One of the men said, "We're going to blindfold you and tie your hands now, so don't try anything."

"Okay," Frank said.

"Okay," Joe repeated.

This wasn't the time to try to escape, Frank decided. What he was hoping was that their captors would lock him and Joe together in a room somewhere so they could make plans.

Once the Hardy boys were blindfolded, the sliding side door of the panel truck opened. Someone took hold of each of their arms and led them across cement.

Joe could smell exhaust fumes. They must be in an underground parking garage, he decided.

Frank heard a dinging sound, and he knew that they were standing in front of an elevator. He was proven right when he recognized the sound of elevator doors whooshing open.

For some reason, Joe thought, *elevators smell the same all over the world, and after the doors close, you feel as though you're in a soundproof room.*

From the rapid ascent, Frank was sure that this was a private elevator that only stopped at the top floors of the building. He wondered what kind of building they were in. Was it the headquarters of some company, or was it one of the high-rise apartment buildings in downtown Philadelphia? It occurred to him that they might soon be involved in another robbery.

When the elevator stopped and the doors opened, Joe felt a hand on his back push him out. Once again someone grabbed his arm and led him through wherever they were.

Frank knew they were standing in front of a door and that someone was using a key. In his mind he wondered if they were about to meet someone even higher up than the baron.

When the door opened, the Hardy boys were pushed inside.

"Take off your blindfolds," a man said.

Joe was stunned. He recognized the voice. The last thing he wanted was to take off his blindfold and look at the person standing before them.

Frank slowly removed his blindfold and blinked. As his eyes focused, he said, "Why did you do it, Mario?"

Mario Zettarella gave him a steely stare. "For the

130

money," he said. "Why else do people break the law?" He shook his head. "Yesterday, I told the baron that he had to cut me in on his operation or I'd send him to prison. When he agreed, I knew I had to find a way to get rid of you two, because you were getting too close to the truth."

Yesterday? Frank thought. *That means this whole operation today was a setup!*

Joe angrily removed his blindfold. "You're sworn to uphold the law!" he shouted at Mario.

Mario snorted. "Don't give me platitudes," he said. "People don't respect the police. We can't make a decent living."

"Our father trusted you," Frank said.

"Well, that's too bad," Mario said. He shook his head. "If it hadn't been for Elisabeth, you two would be at the bottom of the Atlantic, but she managed to convince her father to countermand my orders, and now—well, here you are, and I have to figure out another way to deal with you."

"I'm sure you'll think of something," Joe said sarcastically.

"Oh, yes, I'm sure I will," Mario said. "This will be the final case for the Hardy boys." He stood up. "I've got some other business to take care of. Enjoy your last few hours."

14 Escape!

"Greed," Joe said after Mario was gone. "It's all about greed." He shook his head in disgust. "We could sit here all day and analyze the reasons why Mario really did this, Frank, but we'd better focus on finding a way out of here," he said. "We probably don't have long. I'm sure Mario is just trying to figure out some way to get rid of us that won't tie him to the crime."

"It's Elisabeth who puzzles me. For some reason, she convinced the pilot to fly us here," Frank said. "I wonder why."

Joe walked over to the window and looked out. "Frank! Come here!"

Frank joined Joe at the window. "What's the matter?" he asked.

"Does any of this look familiar?" Joe said.

Frank looked at the buildings across the street, then he said, "Joe! We're in Elisabeth's apartment building!"

"I think we're probably in her *apartment*," Joe said. "I remember smelling something familiar when we got here, and I think it was her perfume."

"It's all right! My father wants me to talk to them!"

A girl's voice had come from the other side of the door, and the Hardy boys immediately recognized it as Elisabeth's. There was a click, and the door opened. Elisabeth stood there, a scowl on her face. Behind her was a burly guard. "Don't worry. They're not going anywhere," Elisabeth said. "I just want to find out what they know."

At that, Elisabeth stepped inside the room and closed the door behind her. She immediately put a finger to her lips, letting Frank and Joe know that they shouldn't say anything. It also told them that maybe, just maybe, they had a chance to escape.

"Well, well, I guess the mighty Hardy boys have met their match," Elisabeth said melodramatically, and loud enough for the guard to hear her.

But Frank could see in Elisabeth's eyes that she didn't mean a word of it.

When she got to Frank and Joe, she whispered, "I'm sorry, and I'm going to help you get out of here, but it's not going to be easy."

133

"Did you really radio the pilot to bring us back here?" Joe asked.

Elisabeth nodded. "Nobody was supposed to get hurt. It was only about robbing people's apartments," she said. "Not murder!"

"If you help us escape, Elisabeth, we'll make sure the police know what you did," Joe said, encouraging her. She was clearly their last hope. "It'll make a difference."

Elisabeth shook her head. "This just all got out of hand," she said. Now there were tears in her eyes.

"How did Mario get involved?" Frank asked.

"He's shrewd. He's very shrewd," Elisabeth said. "He suspected Aérocirque after the first robbery in New York, so he watched us carefully here in Philadelphia, and late yesterday he told my father what he wanted."

"Blackmail," Joe said.

Elisabeth nodded.

"Is everything all right in there?" the guard called.

"Yes, yes, it's fine," Elisabeth shouted back, in a tough, angry voice. "I'm getting what I need for my father. Don't worry about me. I can take care of myself." Under her breath, she added, "We need to hurry."

"Just tell us how we can get out, and we'll do it," Joe said. He hesitated. "Why don't you come with us? When they find out what you've done, there's no telling what they'll do to you."

"I've got this all planned out. They'll never guess that I had anything to do with it," Elisabeth said. "You're going to walk a rope to the building across the street."

Frank and Joe looked at each other.

"Are you serious?" Joe said. "That's your plan?"

"You did it once, and there's no reason why you can't do it again," Elisabeth said. "It's the only way out. There are guards everywhere, but they'll never suspect this."

"Why wouldn't they?" Frank said. "You said it yourself. We did it once, so why wouldn't we do it again?"

"That's just the point. I overheard Mario talking to my father. He didn't think you'd make it across the first time," Elisabeth said. "When you did, he was sure you'd fall the second time. I don't think anyone will expect you to try it a third time."

"When we saw Mario here, I just didn't want to believe that the whole thing was a setup," Frank said. "It's just too . . . *evil.*"

"Mario thought it would be an easy way to get rid of you without anyone suspecting the truth," Elisabeth said. "He was sure that the daring Hardy boys would go along with it, thinking it was the only way to make sure the Aérocirque acrobats were caught so the robberies would stop."

"Mario gave us a little black wire to communicate with him so that he would know which apartment was going to be robbed. The plan was for him and his officers to be there to catch the acrobats when they came across the rope," Frank said. "So something else I already suspected must be true: That wire was a phony. We were just supposed to *think* we were communicating with him."

Elisabeth nodded. "That was an added incentive. If you believed you were in contact with Mario, you'd be more likely to walk the rope," Elisabeth said. "When you both fell, as Mario was sure you would, he would have been a witness to the bravery of the Hardy boys as they tried to solve another baffling case."

"Frank and I were concerned about all the noise—that it would keep Mario from learning our position," Joe said, "when all along he knew where we were headed."

"I dropped the radio after we jumped from the helicopter, but Mario and his officers showed up anyway," Frank said. "At the time, it seemed a little strange, but Mario had an explanation for it—so we shook it off."

"I'm sorry," Elisabeth said. She looked nervously toward the door. "You have to go now!"

Frank looked at Joe. "It's the only way out," he said. "We have no other choice."

Joe nodded. "You're right," he said. He turned to Elisabeth. "Serge used a small rocket launcher to get the rope to the other building," he told her. "How are we going to do that?"

Elisabeth smiled. "Where do you think they store all of their equipment?" she said.

She walked over to the bookcase, removed a large volume from one of the shelves, and stuck her hand through the space where the book used to be. Within seconds the bookcase opened, revealing a large walk-in safe.

"If this were a movie, I'd have expected something like this," Joe said. "I guess this whole thing from beginning to end's been like a movie, though, so I'm not surprised!"

Elisabeth opened the thick door, turned on a light, and Frank and Joe followed her inside.

There were small rocket launchers, piles of rope, and grappling hooks stacked all over the floor.

"Why so much?" Frank asked.

"When they were in a hurry to get away with what they stole from the different apartments, the acrobats had to leave their equipment behind," Elisabeth explained. "It can't be traced, so that's no problem, but we had to keep them supplied. My father's job in the plan is to take what they'll

137

need to each performance, so they'll have it."

"Does Mario know about this?" Joe said.

"He knows about the equipment, certainly, but he doesn't know about this room," Elisabeth said. She smiled at them. "He'll have no idea how you were able to escape."

"What about your father? What will he do when he finds out we've escaped?" Frank asked. "Will he suspect you?"

Elisabeth hesitated for a moment, then she said, "My father has already left the country. He flew out on his private jet to an island in the Caribbean a couple of hours ago. No one knows he's gone. Mario thinks he's with the Aérocirque acrobats, planning another robbery for tonight."

Joe frowned. "And you stayed behind?" he said. "Why?"

"I told you," Elisabeth said. "Murder was never a part of this plan."

"If you can sacrifice your safety for us, we can do our part to make sure these people are brought to justice," Frank said. "Joe and I'll get out of here, and since I don't know who in the Philadelphia Police Department we can trust, we'll bring back the FBI—but I want you to leave the apartment as soon as you can."

"Why?" Elisabeth said.

"You won't be safe when they find out what's

happened," Joe said, "and Mario may already know that your father has left the country."

"I'll tell the guards I'm going shopping, something they won't find hard to believe," Elisabeth said, "and then I'll wait for your call on my cell phone."

"That sounds like a plan," Frank said.

Elisabeth looked at them both. "Are you sure you can make it across?" she asked.

Frank nodded. "The Hardy boys can do anything they put their minds to," he said.

"I believe that," Elisabeth said.

She helped Frank and Joe carry the rocket launcher, the rope, and the grappling hook over to the window.

"That middle building across the street looks like a good bet," Joe said. "The metal barrier on the roof is about level with this floor, so I say we make that our destination."

"I agree," Frank said. He looked around the room. "What'll we anchor the rope to in here?"

"The door to the safe," Elisabeth said. "It won't budge."

"Good idea," Joe said.

Frank aimed the launcher toward the metal barrier on the roof and pulled the trigger. With lightning speed, the grappling hook and rope shot across the distance and locked around one of the metal bars.

"Now let's tie this end to the safe door, and we'll be ready for our performance," Frank said.

With Elisabeth's help, Frank and Joe soon had the rope anchored to the safe door and as taut as they could make it.

Frank took off his shoes but left on his socks. Joe followed suit. This time they meant business.

"Now, for the performance of our lives," Joe said. He climbed up on the window frame and tested the rope. "There's more give than I'd like, but it'll have to do." Slowly, he stepped onto the rope. When he felt he was balanced, he started across.

"Wait, Joe! I'm scared! Maybe we can come up with a different plan of escape!" Elisabeth suddenly said, her voice full of concern. "There must be another way!"

Frank saw Joe falter for just a minute, then regain his balance and continue sliding his feet along the rope.

Frank shook his head. "We'll make it, Elisabeth," he said. "You were right the first time. This is the only way out." Frank climbed onto the window frame, ready to step out onto the rope when Joe was several more feet away. "You hurry up and leave, but say something to make the guard believe we're still inside."

"Okay. I have total faith in the Hardy boys," Elisabeth said. "I'm sorry for whatever role I played in this, but I know everything will be all right, and I'll see you soon."

"Soon," Frank said as he stepped out onto the rope. "Soon," he repeated. He certainly hoped he and Joe could keep that promise.

15 A New Circus Act?

It was almost dawn, but the street below Joe hadn't yet come alive with early morning traffic. That was a good thing, Joe told himself. That meant he and Frank could probably make it across to the other building without attracting unwanted attention.

Frank was trying to stay far enough behind Joe that he wouldn't sway the rope too much. It wasn't as taut as it should be, he knew, and he was hoping that the rope wasn't pulling loose from the door of the safe.

Just a few more feet, Joe thought, and he'd be at the next building. At first, when he thought about what he and Frank were doing, he was amazed and just a little bit, well . . . frightened, but he was able to stay calm by reminding himself that this was similar to some of the things he and Frank did in gymnastics when they were training for competition. In fact, just a couple of weeks ago during one of the sessions, their coach had brought in a friend of his who was on the United States Olympic Committee, and the man had told Joe that if he kept at it, he could make the team in 2008. Just the memory of that fired him up with enough adrenaline to keep going.

Frank was glad that Joe was almost to the building. When his brother finally reached the metal barrier, Frank was prepared to speed up his trip across. He thought he could move just a little faster once he was the only one on the rope.

Suddenly Frank heard a commotion behind him. He was sure it was coming from the room they had just left. He couldn't look around, because he might lose his balance. But something inside his head told him that he needed to move faster, even if it made Joe's trip less steady. He was sure that his brother would compensate in some way.

"Hurry, Frank!" Elisabeth screamed. "Hurry . . ."

Joe had heard Elisabeth's piercing scream at Frank, but the rest of what she said was muffled, and he was sure that somebody had his hand around her mouth to keep her from saying anything else. He slid his feet faster along the rope. It was getting harder to balance because the rope now had more slack in it. Just then the rope lost all of its tautness—but at the last minute, Joe grabbed the side of the building and started pulling himself onto the roof.

Moments earlier, Frank knew someone had discovered that they had escaped, and he was certain that Elisabeth was doing her best to make sure they still made it across—but given the slack in the rope, he was sure, too, that it would be a losing battle. Frank could see that Joe had made it across and was now on the roof, so he no longer had to worry about upsetting his brother's balance—but could he manage to . . . ?

Suddenly, Frank was in free fall. Someone had cut the rope loose.

At the last minute, Frank grabbed hold of the rope and was soon flying toward the building across the street. In seconds, he slammed against the bricks. The impact nearly jarred him loose from the rope, but somehow he managed to hang on.

"Frank! Frank!"

Frank slowly raised his head. Among the stars he was still seeing, he could also make out Joe's face.

"You'll have to climb up the side of the building, but you can do it," Joe called down. "Just pretend we're at camp, and you're climbing those wooden walls on the obstacle course!"

Joe had no doubt that physically, Frank could make it. His brother was tough. The thing that worried him was that he had seen Mario's angry face in the window across the street. There was no telling what he was planning for them now. Just thinking about the possibilities scared Joe. Their father had told them before that the most dangerous criminals are always good men and women who suddenly turn bad. Often, at the end of their short crime spree, when they realize what a mess they've made of their once-exemplary lives, they simply lose all perspective and commit crimes more heinous than those of career criminals.

Frank's arm muscles were beginning to burn, but he knew he was making progress. The salt from his perspiration was getting in his eyes, making it almost impossible for him to see, but he thought he could count five more floors between him and the top of the building. Now it would just be a race against time. He was positive that Mario was on his way over, hoping to capture him and Joe again before they could do any more damage to his short criminal career.

Only two more floors, Frank thought as he used a shoulder to try to wipe the perspiration from his eyes. Above him, he could hear Joe shouting encouragement. *Make yourself think you're back at Bayport High School,* Frank told himself. *You're in competition, and Joe and our parents are cheering you on.* For just a minute that helped, but then he experienced one of the worst muscle cramps in his arms that he had ever had. Taking a minor rest, he started to lose hope. *I'm not going to make it,* he thought.

Just then a window opened.

"Young man! Just what do you think you're doing?"

Frank looked toward the window. "Uh, well, I'm trying to reach the top of this building, ma'am," he managed to say. "You see, my brother's waiting for me, and when I get up there, we're going to go get the FBI."

"A likely story," the woman said. "Anyway, the roof door is locked, and the superintendent has the one key, and he's gone for the day."

"What do you suggest, then?" Frank asked her. He couldn't believe that he was hanging several stories above a Philadelphia street having a weird conversation with this elderly lady.

"Well, if you're just one of those teenagers who likes to pretend he's a comic book character and climb up the side of a building, then I'll let you in—but you're going to have to turn yourselves in to the authorities and take your punishment," the woman said. "If you're a criminal, then you'll just have to find your own way off the roof."

Frank wasn't quite sure how much longer he could hang on, but he thought the elderly woman's faulty logic was a little funny—and it helped him keep going. "I'm one of those goofy teenagers," he managed to say. "It would be great if you could let me and my brother in."

The woman stood aside. "Tell your brother to climb down, then," she said.

Frank looked up. He could tell that Joe had been watching him. "Climb down," he said. "I'll explain later." With that, he swung his body inside the window, put his feet on the floor, and stood up. "Thank you, ma'am," he said.

Joe started down the rope. He had no idea what was going on, but he was sure it wasn't a trap, or Frank would never have gone into the apartment.

When Joe reached the window, Frank was there to pull him inside. Joe then reached back outside, jerked on the rope, and pulled it and the grappling hook into the apartment. "I didn't want to leave any evidence," he said.

"Wise," Frank said. He turned to the woman. "This is Louise Schuster, Joe. She tries to help wayward teenagers, and I told her you and I were really wayward."

"That's right, young man," Louise said. "I've set a lot of young people straight in my time."

Joe was sure she was probably close to a hundred years old. "Yes, my brother and I are really wayward—and we appreciate you setting us straight," he said.

"The door to the roof was locked, so that's why Louise let us in here," Frank said. "I promised her we'd turn ourselves in, so I've already called the FBI."

Over tea and cookies, Louise told Frank and Joe

a shortened version of the complete story of her life. Neither of the Hardy boys was sure how much of it was true, but it still made for an interesting way to pass the time until the FBI arrived.

Once, Frank was sure the commotion he heard outside Louise's apartment was Mario and his officers coming for them, but it turned out not to be. Evidently, none of them had seen him and Joe climb into Louise's window. They were now probably thinking that they had the Hardy boys trapped on the roof.

Within about twenty minutes, two FBI agents arrived.

Frank and Joe motioned the agents away from Louise, and gave the man and woman a quick summary of what had happened. Then they both agreed to go to FBI headquarters in downtown Philadelphia to fill in the rest of the blanks about Aérocirque and Mario Zettarella. Frank and Joe made sure the agents knew that Elisabeth was responsible for saving their lives.

"Thank you again, Louise," Frank said, turning back toward the elderly woman.

"You two try to stay out of trouble, now," Louise told them.

"We'll do our best," Joe said.

By that evening, Mario, two of his officers, and all of the Aérocirque acrobats had been arrested.

Elisabeth was being held too, but one of the agents said he was sure the judge would look kindly on how much she had helped Frank and Joe.

Chet, driving the Hardy boys' van, arrived at FBI headquarters with Matt and Tony. Frank and Joe met them at the curb.

Chet slid over and Frank climbed behind the wheel.

"I'm ready to get back to Bayport," Frank said. He grinned at Joe. "I'm tired of the circus life."

As they headed out of Philadelphia, Joe told them all that had happened during the last few hours.

"I felt really sorry for Gina," Matt said. "Mario rushed in, told her that he had to go on a case out of the country, and started packing a suitcase."

"It wasn't long after that that the FBI arrived," Tony said. "We did our best to console Gina, because she was in hysterics when she found out, but one of her sisters came and took her to her house."

As they crossed into New Jersey, Matt said, "I just thought of something. We're having a student council meeting Monday to try to figure out some way to make a lot of money for some badly needed school projects—and I think I have a really great idea."

"What?" Joe asked.

"You and Frank can perform your high-wire acts

in the gym," Matt said. "We'll charge, and it'll raise a fortune!"

Frank and Joe looked at each other and smirked.

"Well, I guess we were a pretty good act," Joe said. "I mean, we're still here to tell about it."

Frank grinned. "Actually, I'd decided to retire from the circus," he said, "but this sounds like it's for a good cause—so I guess retirement could wait a few days."

"We'll need a name for your act, though," Tony said. He thought for a few minutes. "It has to be good. Something like *The Magnificent Hardys* or *The Flying H Brothers*. But better."

"We could call the show *Hardycirque*," Chet said. "It'll be an annual event!"

"That's it! Hey, who knows?" Matt said. "If you get tired of solving mysteries, you could join a real circus."

"Nah. This is a one-time thing," Frank said. "We'll do it for Bayport High School one last time."

"Agreed," Joe said, smiling. "Then it's back to the usual for us. You know, just performing other death-defying stunts, going undercover, and fighting huge criminals!" With a laugh, Joe playfully punched his brother on the arm.

Wacky things keep happening in
Middleburg–join in the fun with the

By Phyllis Reynolds Naylor

Bernie Magruder and the Case of the Big Stink

Bernie Magruder and the Disappearing Bodies

Bernie Magruder and the Haunted Hotel

Bernie Magruder and the Drive-thru Funeral Parlor

Bernie Magruder and the Bus Station Blow-up

Bernie Magruder and the Parachute Peril

Bernie Magruder and the Pirate's Treasure